SCHOOLGIRL JEN

It was a small metal box, rusted and discoloured.

SCHOOLGIRL JEN AT THE ABBEY

by

ELSIE JEANETTE OXENHAM

COLLINS
LONDON AND GLASGOW

First printed in this Edition 1953
Reprinted   1954
    „   1955

PRINTED AND MADE IN GREAT BRITAIN BY
WM. COLLINS SONS AND CO. LTD.
LONDON AND GLASGOW

CONTENTS

CHAP.		PAGE
I	THE TRAGEDY OF A TREE	7
II	VINNY MILES	16
III	PLANS FOR LAVINIA	22
IV	AN ADVENTURE IN THE ABBEY	28
V	BONIFACE BROWNING	38
VI	A DESCENDANT OF THE MONKS	46
VII	VINNY NOT AT HOME	54
VIII	THE TREE FALLS	60
IX	JEN REMEMBERS	67
X	UNCLE BONNY	77
XI	A VISIT FROM LAVINIA	86
XII	SIR KEITH RINGS UP	96
XIII	A BOOK FOR BABY KAT	102
XIV	ST. FRANCIS IN THE ABBEY	109
XV	VINNY'S MYSTERIOUS BOOK	119
XVI	LETTERS, AND A DIARY	129
XVII	JANE'S SECRET HOUSE	138

5

CHAP.		PAGE
XVIII	JANE'S SECRET MAP	149
XIX	UNCLE BONNY'S SECRET	156
XX	DISAPPOINTMENT	165
XXI	A FEAST OF REJOICING	174
XXII	JEN'S GREAT IDEA	181
XXIII	DIGGING FOR TREASURE	189
XXIV	BROWN BEADS	199
XXV	SUSIE SPINDLE IN TROUBLE	205
XXVI	A CALL FOR JEN	212
XXVII	DOUBTS OF BONIFACE	218
XXVIII	SUSIE IS SENSIBLE	225
XXIX	THE BABES IN THE WOOD ARE AFRAID	232
XXX	JANDY MAC IS NOBLE	238
XXXI	THE BABES IN THE WOOD SET OUT	246
XXXII	THE BABES IN THE WOOD ARRIVE	254

CHAPTER I

THE TRAGEDY OF A TREE

"WHAT a good thing Jandy Mac didn't come back while you were having measles!" Jen had seen the writing on the letter as she handed it to Joan. "It would have been jolly awkward, wouldn't it?"

Joan looked at her in amusement. "Do you really think we left it to chance, Jenny-Wren? Of course Mother wrote and told Jandy about the measles."

"Oh, I see! She told Jandy to stay in Scotland till you were all right again?"

"She didn't put it that way. She said, if Jandy had to go back to Australia on the day she'd planned, we were afraid we shouldn't see her again, as Joy and I would still be in quarantine. Jandy wrote that she must see us once more, so she would put off her journey and stay with her aunts till we could have her here to say good-bye."

"Because once she goes to Australia and marries her cousin, it may be years before she comes back," Jen agreed. "Is she coming now?"

"She'd like to come, but it's awkward." And Joan looked worried. "Mother wants to take Joy to the sea for a few weeks, to get braced up before the winter. She really had a very bad time, with pneumonia on top of measles. I know!" as Jen

7

began to speak. "It was her own fault, but that doesn't alter the result. She isn't very fit, and Mother thinks it would do her good to go away."

"Won't you go with them? You had measles too."

"Even if mine was only a very little measle!" Joan laughed. "I wasn't really ill. Mother meant us both to go, but it isn't necessary for me; I'm quite well again. If Mother thinks Joy should go at once, I shall stay to entertain Jandy Mac."

"Don't they want to see her?"

"Terribly much! I'm to keep her here till they come back. Jandy will want to see them too. But Joy really ought to go away."

"I want to see Jandy quite as much as Joy does," Jen argued. "Do you think she'll come before I have to go home?"

She had been caught by the measles quarantine while on a week-end visit to the Hall. Escaping the infection, she had had a glorious mid-term holiday, and had only gone back to school in time to pack for the journey home to Yorkshire. Then a letter from her mother had told of new plans.

"Father and I have to go to Glasgow. Harry's wedding has had to be hurried on; he is going to the States on business for his firm—a sudden arrangement—and he wants to take Alison with him and make it an extra honeymoon. So they are being married at the end of July, instead of in September, and Father and I must be there. It has all been decided in a hurry, and there is no time for you to come home to go with us; we shall be in Glasgow when you get this letter. But we shall stay only for a very few days. I hope you won't be lonely at home for a long week-end! Father wants to look up some old friends in Scotland, as he will be there anyway."

Jen had shown the letter to Joan and Joy rather dolefully. "It doesn't sound too good for me! I'll have nobody to talk to, except the maids and farm people."

"Why not come to us for the long week-end, and go home when your people will be ready to welcome you?" was Joan's instant and natural response, with a quick look at Joy, to whom the house belonged.

"Would you? Oh, would you? But you've had such a lot of me this term!"

"Could we ever have too much of you?" Joan asked gravely.

"I should think you could! Much too much."

"Not of Jenny-Wren," Joy said. "Never too much of Mrs. Wren! Of course she must stay with us."

"I love you, Joy Shirley!" Jen proclaimed.

"I thought it was Joan you loved," Joy teased.

"Joan most, but you too," Jen told her. "You're so frightfully decent about inviting people to your lovely house."

"Can't keep it all to myself," Joy said lightly. But she looked pleased.

The Hall, where Jen was to spend her long

week-end, had come to Joy from her grandfather, Sir Antony Abinger, two years before, but the beautiful Abbey ruins, in the grounds of the Hall, had been left to Joan, her cousin. Joan's mother, Mrs. Shirley, was Joy's trustee and guardian till she came of age; she was not strong, and the anxiety, when Joy's attack of measles developed into pneumonia, had brought on a heart attack which had frightened everybody but Joy, who was too ill to know anything about it. Mrs. Shirley was better now, but Joan felt strongly that her mother, as well as Joy, would be helped by a while at the sea.

So rooms were taken in a big hotel in Bournemouth, and Joy and her aunt made their preparations, Joy keenly excited about this first experience of hotel life, for until she had come into her inheritance their way had lain in very quiet places. Joy was thrilled and delighted, but she promised Joan earnestly that she would take care of Mrs. Shirley and not let her do too much.

"Don't overtire her, trying to see everything in the first few days! I know you, Joy," Joan warned her.

She and Joy were seventeen and had just left school. With their beautiful dark red hair drawn back into long plaits, they looked much more grown-up than fourteen-year-old Jen, who was blue-eyed and had two thick, yellow pigtails. All three were close friends, in spite of the difference in age, and Jen had spent much time at the Hall since coming to the Wycombe school the year before. Her aunt who lived in the town had died during the winter, and Jen had no relatives nearer than Yorkshire. She had promptly adopted Joan's mother as "Aunty Shirley"; she was maid-of-honour to Joan in the May Queen procession, though Joan's reign was now over.

Janice Macdonald, or "Jandy Mac", was a connection of the family, though there was no real relationship. She had come from Australia to make friends, and had spent the summer at the Hall the year before. Returning for a second visit, wearing a ruby engagement ring, she had gone to stay with old aunts in Scotland, but had promised to spend some time with Joan and Joy before going back to Sydney to marry her cousin. The measles quarantine had put off her return, but now she felt she ought to be on her way again.

Jen arrived for her week-end just as Joy and Mrs. Shirley were starting. She stood with Joan on the terrace waving good-bye; then she whirled round, wild excitement in her eyes.

"Now we're all on our own, just you and me, Joan-Queen! Isn't that super? When does Jandy Mac come?"

"To-morrow evening, Jenny-Wren. We'll have one lonely night."

"Not lonely, not you and me! We'll find something lovely to do. You can teach me a new jig. Joan, what did Joy mean by what she said just now?"

"What did she say?"

"She said: 'I'm glad I'm going away. You and Mrs. Wren can face the tragedy together.' There's nothing wrong, is there, Joan?"

Joan's face was grave. "Not wrong, but very distressing. We have to say good-bye to something—to somebody—whom we love rather a lot."

Jen looked startled. "Who? Oh, Joan, not one of the cats? Not the Mother Superior? She's getting rather old! Or the Curate, or Timmy? Tell me, Joan!"

"Not one of the cats." Joan smiled at her. "I hope—oh, how I hope!—that when they have to die they'll go naturally and easily, without having to be put to sleep. I'd hate to need to do that."

"You couldn't do it! Not one of our dear Abbey cats!"

"We might have to do it, if it was better for them. But it isn't a cat this time; they're all extremely well and flourishing. You know the big tree near the gate-house—the great elm?"

"The tree!" Jen exclaimed. "I love that big tree. It shades the gate-house so nicely, as if it were protecting it. I'm sure Ambrose used to sit under it! What about the tree, Joan?"

"If Ambrose sat under it, it was a very much smaller tree," Joan observed. "Ambrose lived four hundred years ago." And her thoughts went to the lay-brother, who had come back to the Abbey after its destruction by Henry the Eighth's men and had lived in the gate-house to a great age, close to the ruins of his monastery, and whose grave Jen herself had discovered far below, in the tunnels under the Abbey.

"Trees live to be hundreds of years old. I'm sure Ambrose sat under our elm," Jen insisted. "What about the tree, Joan?"

"It has to go. Men are coming to cut it down to-morrow morning." Joan told her the bad news quickly.

"Oh, *no*! Oh, Joan, no! You mustn't let them!" Jen cried in anguish. "It would be murder! Who wants you to cut it down? They can't make you do it! It's yours!"

"I feel terribly bad about it," Joan said heavily. "But there's no help for it, Jen. There's something wrong with the tree: a disease that elms have. It's dying, though we hadn't noticed anything wrong. It isn't safe. It might fall suddenly, and some of our tourists might be killed—or one of the cats, or us. It may infect other elms; there are several at the farm next door. We can't keep it when it may do harm."

"Who told you?" Jen had turned away from her and was staring across the lawn with eyes that did not see the beds of glowing asters and marigolds and late roses.

"Mr. Edwards, from the farm, came to see me— old Matthew Edwards."

"The horrid man who quarrelled with Joy, when she went in his fields, and wouldn't say it was all right when she apologised?"

"And so we don't go near the farm," Joan agreed. "He has several fine elms and he doesn't want them to catch the disease. He told me the tree wasn't safe and must come down. I said all I could, but I knew he was right. If you like, we'll go out for the day, up on to the hills, and only come back when it's all over."

"When the murder has been done," Jen said unhappily. "No, it seems mean. If the tree's going to be killed, we ought to stay with it. We might be some comfort to it."

"Oh, Jen!" Joan half-laughed, in spite of her distress.

"I'm sure it's fond of us. It would seem so unkind to go off and have a picnic. The meadow will look awfully bare without it," Jen added.

"We shall get used to it. You know, Jen, it really is too big," Joan urged. "It shadows the gate-house and hangs over the fish-stream. The gate-house is beautiful, although no one pays much attention to it, because they're in such a hurry to get to the Abbey itself; we shall see it much better when the elm has gone. I'd never have said the tree must go, just to give us a better view, but if it has to come down, for safety reasons, I believe once we're used to it we shall find it's an improvement."

"I don't! It will look simply ghastly—so naked!"

"We could plant another, a sapling," Joan began.

"It would be centuries before it was a real tree. Ambrose's tree! It's a horrible idea!"

"You don't know that it was there in Ambrose's time."

"I'm sure it was. It's quite five hundred years old."

"Mr. Edwards said it was probably five or six hundred," Joan admitted. "He thinks it has been there long enough."

"Old pig!" Jen said bitterly. "Why did he need to come interfering with our tree? It's nothing to do with him."

"I'm afraid it is. He wants to save his own elms," Joan explained.

"To-morrow, did you say? I'm going to say good-bye to our tree. Don't come, Joan!" And Jen rushed off across the lawn and down the narrow shrubbery path, through the Abbey ruins, and out to the meadow, where the gate-house stood astride the carriage drive, protected by the giant elm.

CHAPTER II

"I CAN'T see anything wrong with it!" Jen said resentfully, as she walked round the doomed tree.

"Who's there? Who are you?" she cried suddenly, and stood staring in amazement.

A small girl in a red frock was huddled against the massive trunk, in a corner between two big roots. Dark curls hung untidily on her shoulders, which were shaken by bitter sobbing.

Jen stood gazing at her. "I'd better fetch Joan. *I* don't know what to do for the kid! Who is she? And what is she doing here? Of course, anyone can come in as far as this—it's not like the real Abbey."

The road to the gate-house was open to the lane; the door at which tourists had to pay was farther on, in the wall that enclosed the garth and the ruins. Village folk did not use the gate-house meadow, but there was nothing to prevent them, if they wished to enter.

"I say!" Jen stooped over the child. "What's up? Has somebody been unkind to you? What's your name?"

Dark, tear-filled eyes looked up at her in startled dismay. "I'm sorry, Miss Joan—oh, it's not Miss Joan!" as she saw the yellow plaits and blue eyes.

16

"Rather not! Do you know Joan? Do you want to see her? She'll help, if there's anything the matter."

"We used to come here. Her used to teach us. But I was one of the littler ones. Her won't remember me."

"You're not a very big one yet, are you? What did Joan teach you? I haven't heard about that."

"Drill. Sometimes here and sometimes on the garth. I liked coming to her class."

"I bet you did! I'm sure it was fun. I shall make Joan tell me about it. But who are you? And what's the matter with you?"

The child turned to the tree again, and her thin arms reached up the trunk. "They be a'goin' to cut her down. I heard 'em say it. 'Tis a shame!"

"Oh!" Jen said slowly, and stood staring at her. "I feel just like that myself. But how awfully nice of you to care so much!"

"Miss Joan used to sit here and tell us stories and talk to us. And we had games, touch-last and things like that, and the tree was 'home'. I doesn't want the men to take her away."

"Neither do I, and neither does Joan. But it can't be helped. Mr. Edwards says it isn't safe," Jen explained. "You wouldn't like it to fall on you, you know."

"Mr. Edwards, he told Mr. Jaikes. I heard 'im."

"And you ran away to the tree and howled,"

Jen said, with quick understanding. "I felt like that, too. But it's no use ; we can't save the tree. We can be sorry, but we can't do anything about it."

"How sensible!" she thought ruefully. "I didn't feel sensible when I rushed away from Joan. It's terribly odd! Finding this kid crying her eyes out has made me see how silly it is. What's your name?" she asked again. "I shall have to tell Joan about you."

"Lavinia Miles, please, miss."

"Lavinia!" Jen grinned. "The whole of it, all the time? I'm just Jen; there couldn't be a much littler name than mine. What do they call you? Vinny?"

"Mrs. Jaikes, she calls me Vinny. The boys calls me Lav. I hates it!" And Lavinia flushed resentfully.

"I should think so! But Vinny is rather nice. Vinny Miles, did you say? You don't come from Miles's farm, up in the hills, do you?"

"King's Bottom Farm. I comes to village for school."

"King's Bottom Farm!" Jen said slowly. "I've heard something—yes, I remember. It was John Miles, of King's Bottom, who gave the old maps to Jandy Mac's Uncle Tony, and Jandy showed them to us, and we found the tunnels and the highwayman's treasures and dear old Ambrose's grave. But the Miles people went to America ten years ago, Joy told us, and the farm was sold to

Mr. Jaikes. Did they leave you behind when they went?"

"Yes, miss." Lavinia sat and stared at her. "My mum died, and I were only two; I'm twelve now. My dad didn't know what to do 'bout me; the rest were boys and could look arter themselves. My aunty didn't go to 'Merica, and she said as how she'd keep me here till they got settled down and dad found a job. She went on living at the farm to help Mrs. Jaikes. Then she died, and my dad di'n't want me; he'd got married to somebody in 'Merica. And Mrs. Jaikes, she don't want me neither, for she's got kids of her own. But I hadn't anywheres to go, so I lives at the farm. I helps her quite a bit."

"I'm sure you do," Jen said warmly. "I expect you're very useful to her. But your new mother in America ought to have you. Does she know you're stuck here, left on Mrs. Jaikes's hands?"

"I d'n know, Miss Jen. Mrs. Jaikes said as how she were goin' to write, but I d'n know if she done it."

"You couldn't do it yourself. Not without help," Jen said thoughtfully. "But somebody could help you. Your father ought to send for you. I shall talk to Joan. Are you so frightfully fond of our tree, Vinny?"

"I loves her," Vinny said simply. "Because of Miss Joan sittin' under her, like."

"Joan could sit somewhere else, if that's all.

I expect you've been missing her class, haven't you?"

"Yes, miss. But she hasn't no time for us now."

"I don't suppose she has. She's been terribly busy at school. But she might make time now. Are there other girls who want her classes to go on?"

"No," Vinny said bitterly. "They doesn't care: it's on'y me. They says as how we gets enough lessons at school. We got a new teacher, and she gives us drill, and they says it's plenty."

"They would," Jen agreed. "If it's only you, Vinny Miles, I'm afraid Joan can't have a drill class for one."

"Teacher at school don't tell us stories, like Miss Joan did. She ain't got the time."

"It would do you good just to talk to Joan and try to say things as she does," Jen remarked. "Now, Lavinia, listen to me! It's no use howling about things that are finished, like those classes, or things that have to happen, like the tree. That's finished too, though it's horrible to think of. You came to say good-bye to the tree—it's what I came to do myself—and you've done it. Now you mustn't cry any more; you mustn't be silly. I'll tell Joan about you, and perhaps she'll think of something that will help; and you'll go home to Mrs. Jaikes and the children, and you won't howl any more. You will be sensible, won't you?"

There was adoring gratitude in the look Lavinia gave her. No one, except Joan, had ever taken trouble about her in this wholesale way before.

"I'll do it, Miss Jen."

"Good! Then I'll go and talk to Joan. She may think of some way to help. Your father ought to look after you now. It's silly that you should be dumped on poor Mrs. Jaikes, when you've a father and brothers in America. You ought to go to them. Perhaps Joan will help you to write a letter. I'll see what I can do about it. Off you go! You can't save the tree by clutching hold of it. Good-bye! I expect I'll see you again. If I've gone home, there will still be Joan, and she's much more use than I am."

She watched Lavinia as she ran to the entrance and along the lane. Then, with a grave look at the tree, standing majestic and patient, unconscious of its fate, she raced off in the opposite direction, through the Abbey ruins, to find Joan still sitting on the terrace.

CHAPTER III

PLANS FOR LAVINIA

"I REMEMBER Vinny Miles!" Joan exclaimed, when Jen had told her story at express speed. "She was a small child, who came with the older girls, and seemed to enjoy herself. I never heard her called Lavinia! It sounds like a gipsy."

"A gipsy? I thought it sounded rather stately, like a duchess or a countess," Jen said. "And she's such a scrap of a kid. I nearly laughed in her face."

"The Lady Lavinia—well, perhaps," Joan agreed. "Either that or a gipsy girl. Nice of her to care so much about our tree!"

"It was because you sat under it and told them stories. Tell me about your class, Joan-Queen! I've never heard of it before."

"It was while we lived in the Abbey, as care-takers, before Joy's grandfather took any notice of us. I heard the village girls grousing because they didn't have enough drill at school; their teacher was elderly, and she didn't care about drill. There's a new one now who is very keen, I believe. I invited the girls to come to the Abbey in the evening, and we had quite good times. I'd often thought I'd like to be a gym and games mistress, so it was good practice."

"You'd do it jolly well. Did you drill them on the garth?"

"Sometimes. But sometimes we used the meadow and Joy played for us: we could hear her piano, if we were just outside the windows. The girls liked it best with music, of course. If I'd known about country dancing, they'd have liked that even better than drill. But that was before we met the Hamlet Club and learned to dance. Sometimes we played team games out on the meadow."

"And the big tree was ' home '. You sat under it, and you told them stories."

"I believe I did," Joan said, much amused. "Apparently Lavinia hasn't forgotten."

"She's keen on you. Couldn't we help her somehow ? In a sort of way, she came to the Abbey to be comforted, and she needs help. The monks would have done something about it, wouldn't they?"

"They'd have helped anybody who was in trouble. Vinny Miles seems to be left stranded by her family. What shall we do, Jenny-Wren?"

"I thought you could help her to write a letter to her father. Perhaps one of the brothers could come and fetch her."

"Perhaps the stepmother doesn't want her. But we could try."

"She couldn't possibly do it alone. Her grammar's awful, and I expect her spelling's worse."

"I wonder if she knows the address? But Mrs. Jaikes will have it, and she'd probably be glad to be rid of Vinny. Poor kid! It's dreadful for her. We'll try to help, Jen."

"Oh, good! I knew you would," Jen said happily. "And, I say, Joan! There's one thing we could do at once."

"Oh? What's that, Mrs. Wren?"

"Give her a bit of ribbon and make her tie back her hair. It's fearfully untidy. Having her hair all over the place like that must make her feel an absolute mess!"

"Do you mean, in her mind, as well as in looks?" Joan asked seriously.

Jen gave her a quick glance. "You do understand! I did mean that. She must feel neglected and untidy, going about all hairy. It can't be good for her."

"I'm sure you're right. We'll find a ribbon and present it to Lavinia."

"A bright red ribbon!" Jen pleaded. "She'll love it. Her frock's red."

Joan looked at her and grinned suddenly. "Not one in our house, my dear! It's the last place in the world to find a scarlet hair-ribbon. *Did* you suppose either Joy or I would have one?"

Jen's eyes went to the thick plait of deep red, which lay on Joan's shoulder. "No, I guess not. You'd look awful in scarlet; it would spoil you altogether."

"Mother hasn't any red ribbons, either. We'll

buy one for Lavinia. Do you know what I think? We'll go to see Mrs. Jaikes to-morrow morning. That won't feel like having a picnic."

Jen looked at her quickly again. "While those men—yes, I see. You don't think we ought to stay—with the tree, you know?"

"No, Jenny-Wren, I don't. It was a kind thought, but we couldn't help the tree by being here, and we should feel very bad if we watched. We'll do something to help Vinny Miles, who loves the tree. That will be far better than staying here and feeling sad and sentimental."

"I shall feel sad all right, but I'd hate to do the other thing," Jen said vigorously.

"Then we won't think too much about it. The tree has to go, and there's nothing we can do by being here. To-morrow we'll explore the hills and find our way to Miles's farm and interview Mrs. Jaikes. We might hunt for Vinny's red ribbon in the village. If we can't find any there, we'll walk over the hills to Wycombe and have lunch and buy our ribbon, and then come home by bus."

"And to-night we'll be on our own—just you and me together. It's rather fun, you know, Joan-Queen."

"You ought to stop calling me that, now that Muriel is Queen."

"I'm not going to stop. You're still my Queen. What shall we do to-night? Let's be mad, for once, because we're all alone!"

"I don't think I know how to be mad," Joan said, much amused. "Do you mean pillow-fights? Or hide and seek in the dark, and jumping out on one another with wild shrieks and yells? We'll send for Jacky-boy. She'd help you to be mad better than I should."

Jack, or Jacqueline, had been Jen's chum for a year, since Jen's first day at school. But her home was in Wycombe, and she had just gone off to the seaside with her mother.

"We can't have Jack," Jen said. "But I don't want her. It's being on our own, just us two, that is so thrilling. We could have supper in the Abbey, Joan. That would be a thing we couldn't possibly do while your mother and Joy were here."

"By all means!" Joan was quite willing. "We'll pack a picnic supper and carry it to the Abbey. I'll warn Ann Watson, so that she won't think we are ghosts."

"Perhaps the ghosts of Ambrose and Lady Jehane will come and peep at us." Jen referred to the lay brother and his lady-love, who were part of the Abbey story at the time of its destruction by Henry the Eighth. "I wish they would! I'd love to see them, even their ghosts."

"You'd better not hope for that." Joan laughed, glad to see Jen's thoughts had turned from the doomed tree. "But I can tell you who will expect to share our supper."

"The cats! The Mother Superior and Gray

Timmy and the Curate. We'll take extra milk and some fish."

"You can carry the fish. Come and have some tennis. We must practise, for Jandy will want to play. She'll beat both of us together, I'm quite sure. We haven't had much tennis lately, thanks to the measles, and then Joy's and mother's packing. We'd better do a little work before Jandy comes."

"I'm not much good, but I'll try to give you some sort of game. Cricket's more in my line."

"You must polish up your tennis, while you're here," Joan said, and led her round the house to the courts.

CHAPTER IV

AN ADVENTURE IN THE ABBEY

"IT IS FUN to have you all to myself, Joan-Queen!"
Jen gave Joan a beaming look as they crossed
the garden and entered the Abbey by the old
gate, laden with bags and baskets for the picnic
supper.

The cat family came leaping to greet them:
the slim young Curate, with his square of white
under his chin, his comfortable black mother, and
Timmy, the shaggy gray kitten, now almost full
grown.

"They're pleased to see us," Jen remarked.
"They don't know yet that I'm lugging a bowl
of fish and three extra saucers."

"They'll be still more pleased when they find
it's a feast. Where shall we sit?" Joan paused and
looked round the cloister garth in the evening
light.

"Just outside the chapter-house. We'll see the
sunset from there. I'll fetch a rug." And Jen put
down her basket and went to the little room in
which she had slept for one exciting night.

She came back laden with rugs and cushions
and spread them on the grass, to the delight of the
cats, who at once took possession and made
themselves at home, tramping up and down and

trying place after place. "What a good thing people can't come in here at night! We must look funny, camping out."

"We certainly don't look like a monastery," Joan agreed, laying sandwiches on plates and bringing out thermos flasks of coffee. "Don't touch, children! Yours is coming presently. Where's that fish, Jen?"

"Here. Come on, littlest!" to Timmy. "This is yours, Mother Superior. The Curate last. Now we shall have some peace!" as three hungry faces disappeared into saucers. "It is a feast!" And Jen eyed the display with much satisfaction. "Another adventure for the Abbey! A midnight supper with a Queen!"

"Hardly midnight," Joan objected. "And only an ex-Queen!"

"But we might stay till midnight," Jen hinted. "You can tell me stories, as you used to do to Lavinia and the rest. Let's start! Those sausage rolls make me hungry."

"It may be the tennis. We've brought far too much. We shall go home laden with food."

"Oh, you never know! The cats will help. And I might eat three times as much as usual, because we're out of doors. Or we may find another stowaway, like Timothy Spindle, when I slept over there. I was jolly glad I had some grub to give him."

"I hope there are no more stowaways," Joan said. "But we can present our extra food to Ann

Watson, if there's much left. The family won't care for sausage rolls."

"There's the robin, too. He loves the garth. We could give him our crumbs."

"You can't have Robin and the Curate at the same party," Joan remarked.

"We'll put the Curate to bed and leave crumbs for Robin's breakfast. Aren't they enjoying themselves? They think midnight feasts are a lovely idea. I shall put the crumbs in the sacristy for Robin. He'll be safer there."

Presently even Jen had eaten as much as she could, and she lay back against Joan, stroking the happy Mother Superior, and refusing to go home to bed. She talked of her brother being married next morning and of the telegram she would send to the family party in Glasgow; of Jandy Mac, travelling from Scotland; of Vinny Miles and the old tree that had to go.

"We must go home," Joan said at last.

"In one minute! I'm going to wander round by moonlight. You stay here—unless you want to come too?"

"I'll pack the baskets." And Joan set to work.

"The Curate's gone for his evening prowl, and Timmy's fast asleep: he's had too much supper. I shall have to go alone." And Jen disappeared, running up the steps to the dormitory, torch in hand. Presently she came back to the garth and wandered round the corner to the sacristy, to look at the rose window, which Joy loved so much, and to scatter crumbs for Robin's breakfast.

With a wild cry she came racing back, and flung herself into Joan's arms. "Oh, Joan! Joan! I saw Ambrose—in the sacristy! Oh, Joan, there couldn't be a ghost! But I did see him!"

"Jen, dear, what are you talking about?" Joan cried, and held her tightly. "Why, Jen, you're shaking all over! What startled you, my dear?"

"Ambrose!" Jen sobbed, and hid her face. "An old man, with a long white beard. It couldn't be Ambrose, Joan! But I saw him!"

"It couldn't be Ambrose. There are no such things as ghosts," Joan said firmly. "If you saw anybody, it was someone who has no right to be there. Are you sure it wasn't just a trick of moonlight?"

"Certain sure. He was sitting in the rose window. He got up and came——"

"Wait a moment." Joan put her down, considerably startled herself.

Jen looked up and then sprang to her feet. "There—you see? Ambrose!"

"Not Ambrose," Joan repeated. "Definitely not. But perhaps another stowaway, Jenny-Wren. I wonder if he's in trouble too?"

"A refugee," Jen murmured, and crept forward behind Joan.

An old man stood in the gap in the wall which led to the sacristy and the site of the great church.

He was bent and his eyes were tired; he had a long white beard, and he wore a big brown cloak wrapped round him, but no hat.

"I don't blame Jen. He might very well be an old monk." The thought flashed through Joan's mind as she went to meet him.

"Who are you? And why are you in the Abbey at this time? Why, it's Mr. Browning, isn't it? Mr. Boniface Browning?"

"Yes, Miss Joan. It be I, old Browning. I'm right vexed I scared the little one." The voice was old and tremulous.

"I'm not a little one!" Jen cried indignantly. "And you looked just like the ghost of old Ambrose. Joan, who is it? You know him, and he knows you."

"It's Mr. Browning, who used to be the caretaker and show people round, before Mother took on the job," Joan said swiftly. "He taught me all about the Abbey—all that was known in those days. There's a lot more now. We hadn't heard of Ambrose or found the crypt, or the tunnels, or the Abbey treasures. But you went away to live with your son in Birmingham," she said to Mr. Browning. "What are you doing here? And why are you in the Abbey at night? What was Ann Watson thinking of?"

"I came back for two-three days to see folks again and to bide in the village. The Spindles at the forge took me in."

A quick look flashed from Jen to Joan. "The

Spindles! Timothy Spindle was my first stow-away," Jen murmured.

"But why are you in the Abbey at night?" Joan's tone was severe.

"I came in with a party, late-ish like, to have another look at the old place," he said apologetically. "She didn't know me—the lady who showed us round."

"No, she wouldn't know you," Joan agreed. "You'd been gone for quite two years before Mrs. Watson came here. Did you stay behind when the rest of the party left?"

"I did that, Miss Joan. Mrs. Watson didn't notice I weren't there, and I says a word to the folks when we was down in the old church. 'Don't say nothing,' I says. 'I knows this place, and I'm stopping behind to have another look,' I says. They thought it was all right, so they went away, and she locked the gate and never knew I were still here. There's some queer-like bits down there, Miss Joan. I never knew about them dark places."

"None of us knew. Did you want to explore them by yourself?"

"Have you been wandering in the tunnels on your own?" Jen cried. "You might easily have found the one that leads to the house! What a shock we'd have had, if you'd risen suddenly from the depths of the earth!"

"Mrs. Watson, she said not to go that way, for it went to Miss Joy's house. You beant Miss Joy."

And he eyed Jen severely. "You a'n't big enough, and you're the wrong colour."

"My hair, you mean," Jen grinned. "Mine isn't nearly as lovely a colour as Joan's and Joy's. I'm only staying here, and I'm three years younger than they are. You gave me an awful fright, you know! I don't believe in ghosts, but I really thought you were good old Ambrose, come to speak to us."

"The old one the lady told us about, what lived down there?"

"Who's buried down there," Jen corrected him. "Ambrose lived in the gate-house, after the Abbey was smashed up by that pig, Henry the Eighth. *I* found his grave," she ended proudly.

"Did you, now? The lady showed us. I'm sorry, little miss; I didn't mean to frit nobody. I just wanted to wander about by myself. I was fond of the Abbey." He turned to Joan in apology again. "I never meant no harm, Miss Joan. I was sorry to go away, and I wanted to see the old place once more. And there was so much that I'd never heard tell of. I just felt I'd like to think about it all."

"But what were you going to do in the morning?" Jen cried.

"I'd ha' told her then and asked her to let me out. I ain't done no harm to the place."

"You'd have been very cold and hungry before the morning!"

Joan had been listening in silence. Now she said, "Did you bring any supper?"

"I never thought to do it, Miss Joan."

"Then come and finish ours. We've had a picnic, and there's still some food left and a whole flask of coffee that we couldn't drink. We said we had far too much. We can't have people being hungry in the Abbey."

She led the way back to their resting-place and told the old man to sit on the rug.

With dancing eyes Jen brought a cushion for his back and made him lean against the wall, and supplied him with sandwiches and coffee, using the top of the flask for a cup.

"It's still hot. Don't drop it! There! Are you comfy? Can I get you anything else?"

"Are you pretending he's Ambrose, Jenny-Wren?" Joan spoke in a low voice, unheard by the old man. "He's a little deaf," she explained. "*Were* you, Jen?"

Jen laughed. "Perhaps I was, in a way. He looks quite like Ambrose may have looked."

"He does. Finish up those sandwiches and biscuits, Mr. Browning; they're all for you. We don't want to take them home."

"What's become of the Mother Superior and Timmy?" Jen looked round for the rest of the party.

"They fled when you came shrieking from the sacristy. I expect they thought you were a ghost."

"Well, Joan! Hadn't I some excuse?"

"You had," Joan agreed. "I don't blame you, really. Come over here!"

She crossed the garth, Jen following eagerly, and paused at the door of the little room from which the rugs and cushions had come, and flashed her torch about. "What are we going to do with Ambrose, Jen?"

Jen's eyes sparkled. "I do believe he's Ambrose come back! What a marvellous idea! What can we do? We can't let him wander about the Abbey all night. There's no place that's really warm, is there?"

"Was he in the sacristy? It was a good choice; it isn't so draughty in there. But we can do better than that. He must come here and lie on the bed. We'll spread the big quilt and he can use the heavy rug to cover himself. That will keep him warm and cosy. He won't expect us to make up the bed for him."

"How lovely of you, Joan! Then you aren't going to fling him out or row him for trespassing?"

"Well, what do you think? He was fond of the Abbey, and he was sent away because he was too old. He wanted to see it again. Can we turn him out?"

"Of course we can't! And we don't want to, either. I'm sure the monks would have taken him in. What is it that's written on the gate-house? ' Gate open be, To honest folk all free '? Isn't that what the Latin means?"

"Something like that. Yes, he must stay for to-night. This will do very well. I'll explain to Ann Watson, in case she has a bad fright. He can make his peace with her in the morning."

"She must give him breakfast. She gives jolly good breakfasts," Jen said, from experience.

"I'll tell her he doesn't need anything till the morning. You go and talk to him again." And Joan went along the cloisters to the door of Ann Watson's rooms.

CHAPTER V

BONIFACE BROWNING

"BETWEEN Vinny Miles and Ambrose, our family seems to be growing!" Jen said to herself, as she turned to go back to Mr. Browning. "If Lavinia was a little older, and much more beautiful, I might call her Jehane and say she had come back too. But I really can't—not Vinny! She isn't in the least like our dear Lady Jehane."

She sat on the rug beside their guest, tossing back her long yellow plaits. "I say, Mr. Browning! Won't the forge people be worried when you don't turn up? Weren't the Spindles expecting you to go to bed with them?"

"I said to them as how I'd try to stay in the Abbey for the night," the old man explained. "They'll know I be here."

"Oh, I see! We must tell Joan, or she'll think she has to send a message to say you're all right. She thinks of everything for everybody."

He turned to her eagerly. "Will Miss Joan let me stay, little miss? I'll do no harm."

"My name's Jen—Jen Robins. Of course you won't do any harm. And of course she'll let you stay. She couldn't turn you out of the Abbey."

It had seemed to Mr. Browning that Joan not only could, but would, turn him out. His wistful eyes brightened and wandered lovingly over the moonlit garth.

"I were fond o' this place," he murmured. "I never wanted to go, but Sir Antony said it, and I knew the stairs was too much for me. By time I'd took folks up to the dormitory or the refectory I hadn't no breath left to tell 'em about it. But it hurt me bad when I had to go."

"I'm sure it did," Jen said. "It must have been dreadful to have to leave the Abbey."

"Mrs. Shirley and Miss Joan told it all better than what I could do. This Mrs. Watson, she's good too, and she speaks nice, like I never could."

"Mrs. Watson used to be a nurse to a family in London. She had to speak properly, or she'd have lost her job," Jen explained. "She knows how to say things, but sometimes she forgets. But she remembers all right when she's taking people round."

"Very nice, I thought she told it. I never could do it like that. And my asthma was bad, so Sir Antony said as how I'd have to go. Miss Joan lives at the Hall now, don't she?"

"Yes, but it belongs to Joy. Sir Antony was her grandfather, and he left the house to her. The Abbey belongs to Joan."

"They told me that. She's fond of it too. She'll take care of it."

"Oh, she does! She loves every stone of it, and so do I," Jen said earnestly. "Have some more coffee, Mr. Browning. I'll pour it for you. What did Joan call you? There was some other name besides Browning."

"I'm Boniface, little miss. It was my grandfather's name. They used to call me Boney or Bonny."

Jen's eyes were dancing. "What an odd name! I never met it before. Is it Latin? It sounds rather like an old monk. 'Mr. Bonny Browning' is nice; 'Boney' wouldn't do at all. I think it's a lovely name! But I must speak to Joan. Do eat up those biscuits and that bun!"

And she was gone, flying across the garth, while the old man's eyes followed her wistfully.

"Ann, there's somebody in the Abbey. You left him behind when you locked up. I'm not angry; don't look so worried! He wanted to be left behind. But you should have noticed he didn't go out with the other people." Joan, in the caretaker's little room within the walls, was looking round unhappily, while she told Mrs. Watson about Boniface Browning. For some time this had been her home, and she was not reconciled to the changes which had been made by Ann. By Ann's urgent request the beautiful old gray walls had been colour-washed a cheerful pink; the bare stone, said Ann, was all right in the Abbey, but to live with it "gave her the creeps". Joan, anxious for her caretaker's comfort, had let her have her way; if Ann preferred to live surrounded by bright, hard pink, she must be allowed to do so. But for herself, Joan loathed it, and went into the small parlour as seldom as possible, choosing to interview Ann outside or on the garth whenever she could.

"He'll sleep in the small cloister room. We'll send him to bed before we go home," she said. "But you might give him some breakfast and let him come in here for a wash in the morning."

She cut short Ann's apologies and went out, and almost ran into Jen, who came racing to meet her.

"Why, Jen! Is anything wrong with Mr. Browning?"

"Oh, no! He's terribly happy, having a huge supper and looking at the cloisters in the moonlight as if he'd like to eat them too. He loves the Abbey—anyone can see that. But, oh, Joan! Is his name really Boniface? It's too gorgeous for words!"

"I felt like that when I first heard it. It seemed to suit the Abbey so beautifully," Joan agreed. "It really is his name, Jen! But I fancy he's been called Bonny Browning all his life."

"Yes, he said so. It's a shame to spoil it. 'Boney' wouldn't do: he's not a bit thin! 'Bonny' isn't a bad name for him, with those red, round cheeks like withered apples. But his lovely name oughtn't to be spoiled. I shall call him Boniface. It sounds just like a monk! Ambrose should have been called Boniface. What does it mean? Is it a real name, Joan?"

"Oh, yes! It's a very fine old name. I suppose it means Well-Doer—one who does good things."

"Lovely!" Jen sighed happily. "I am so glad he came back to the Abbey! I shall call one of my children Boniface."

"I hope you'll consider his feelings before you do that! Think how he'd be ragged at school!"

"Perhaps it would be mean," Jen admitted.

"I didn't know you had made up your mind to have a family," Joan remarked.

"Didn't you? I'm going to have lots of children —ten, I think—mostly boys. Jack and I talked about it while you were having measles. It was when we trespassed at the Manor, next door, and I said it looked the sort of house that ought to have a lot of children playing in the garden. I said I couldn't be bothered with a family, but since then I've thought it might be rather fun."

"I'm sure it would," Joan responded, with a laugh. "A lot of boys would suit you: you're used to brothers. But don't call one of them Boniface! It would be unkind."

"All right, I won't. I shall want some girls as well—about three, I think—and all the rest boys."

"Oh, Jen!" Joan protested, laughing. "You're going to have a busy life!"

"Some of them could be twins. Twins must be fun! What are you going to do with Boniface, Joan?"

"Send him to bed, and then go home and think about him."

"Oh, right!" Jen said happily. "I suppose it is bedtime."

"It's bedtime for you, anyway." And Joan explained her plans to old Boniface, who brightened up at thought of sleeping in the Abbey once more, and promised not to wander about, but to go to bed and rest.

Jen packed the remains of the picnic and carried the rugs and cushions to the cloister room. "These will keep Boniface nice and warm," she said, dumping them on the bed.

Joan brought the old man to the door. "Goodnight, Mr. Browning. Sleep well! Mrs. Watson will look after you in the morning. Come along, Jen!"

Jen slung a bag over her shoulder and picked up a basket. "I say, Joan! Such a marvellous idea!"

"You're the one for ideas, Mrs. Wren. What now?"

"Couldn't Boniface and Ann Watson get married? Then he could stay in the Abbey for always, and she could do the work."

Joan gave a shout of laughter. "Jen! Oh, poor Ann! He's old enough to be her father, if not her grandfather!"

"People do marry older people," Jen said sturdily. "She's a widow; she might like to have a husband again. I think it's a very good plan."

"I don't, and I'm quite sure Ann wouldn't."

"Then she could adopt him as a grandfather, and he could live with her. He didn't want to go away from the Abbey. He'd love to spend his last days here."

"It's a kind thought," Joan agreed. "But Ann hasn't room for him, Jen. There's only one bedroom. Where would she put him?"

"He could have the little room, where he is now. It would be like the old days, when the monks had an infirmary for aged people and nursed them till they died. It would bring back another bit of the Abbey, if you kept an aged person here, and Boniface is such a darling. Oh, Joan, do think about it in earnest! He'd be so happy!"

Joan was looking startled. "But that little room is my private place—the only bit of the Abbey that I've kept for myself. You wouldn't take it from me, would you?"

"I forgot," Jen said dejectedly. "No, of course not. You must have your own bit of the Abbey. It seemed such a wonderful plan. I thought we were going to have our old folks' infirmary again. But you couldn't. I see that."

Joan knit her brows. The disappointment in Jen's tone was so acute. "Off you go to bed!" she said, as they reached the house after a silent crossing of the lawn. "Don't worry about Mr. Browning. He'll be very comfortable."

"You'll come and tuck me in, won't you?"

"Baby! Yes, all right. I'll be your mother. I'm going to bed too."

She found Jen lying with her hair loose and spread all over the pillow. "Jenny-Wren! Sit up and plait that stuff. You'll be too hot."

"I will, presently. It's plaited all day. I'm giving it a rest. I'm going to cut it off when I have to put it up. I believe it would be curly."

"I'm sure it would. But you'd look quite different."

"It might be an improvement," Jen grinned. "Give yours a rest too, Joan. I like to see it loose."

Joan obligingly unwound her thick plait and shook the dark red locks free. "There! Now I really shall have to go to bed. Are you sure you've had enough supper?"

"Oh, heaps, thank you very much! Didn't Ambrose—I mean Boniface!—love his sandwiches? It was lucky for him we had our picnic to-night!"

"Yes, he'd have been both cold and hungry by the morning. It was a silly thing to do. But he's all right where he is."

"Joan, I'm sorry I made that plan. I forgot it was your bit of the Abbey. I didn't worry you, did I?"

"Of course not, Jenny-Wren. Now do your hair and go to sleep."

"All the same, I believe it did worry her," Jen said to herself, as she sat up to plait her hair, after Joan had gone. "I'm sorry I said it. But it would have been marvellous if Boniface Browning could have been the aged and infirm who stayed in the Abbey for ever and ever! I'm sure he'd have loved it. Oh, well! It can't be done, that's all!"

CHAPTER VI

A DESCENDANT OF THE MONKS

"Jen has forgotten all about the tree," Joan said to herself, as she prepared for bed. "From that point of view, I'm glad Boniface turned up to-night. The picnic alone might not have been enough to distract her thoughts. But I do wish she hadn't put that idea into my head. If only she hadn't sounded so bitterly disappointed! For it would be possible. And it would make the old man very happy. But I don't want to do it."

She sat on the window-seat and stared out at the moonlit lawn. "He has a pension. Ann could feed him and make a little extra for herself. I dare say she'd be pleased. If she liked him, he'd be company for her. But he'd be there always, in the Abbey, wandering in and out. I feel I should lose the Abbey itself, as well as my room—and the room has been really useful. I've gone there a lot, and I've often thought I could lend it to people for an extra bedroom some day. Jen enjoyed sleeping there; and I slept in it myself while the school was here. All that would be over; and the private feeling of the Abbey would be gone. We'd know we might meet old Boniface at any moment. *How* I wish Jen hadn't had that idea!"

Very slowly she went to bed, but lay awake for

a long time, turning over the problem in her mind.

There was only one way out. The Abbey welcome to old and tired folk must be upheld.

Joan dressed quietly early next morning and found, as she expected, that Jen was still sleeping when she glanced into her room. Closing the door gently, she crept downstairs and out into the garden.

Crossing the lawn to the Abbey gate, she went down the tresaunt passage, and paused in the old doorway to look anxiously round the garth. But there was no sign of Boniface, and his door was still closed.

Much relieved, Joan went to Ann Watson's rooms.

"Ann, are you up? I want to talk to you."

"Eh, Miss Joan?" Ann's startled face appeared. "It's early; I'm not very tidy yet. I was getting a bite of breakfast for the old gentleman, in case he comes along."

"That's good of you. I'm sorry to disturb you, but I want to speak to you about Mr. Browning."

Ann hastily dusted a chair. "Yes, Miss Joan? I had a word with him last night, asking if he wanted anything. He seems a nice quiet gentleman, but his breathing's bad, isn't it? Asthma, he says it is."

"Yes, I'm afraid it troubles him a good deal. I'm glad you've spoken to him. Do you like him, Ann?"

Ann looked puzzled. "Well enough, Miss Joan. I'm pleased to do for him this morning."

"Could you do with him for a few days, if I invited him to stay in the Abbey? He could sleep in the small room, if you would give him meals."

"To stay in the Abbey, Miss Joan?" Ann's startled look came back.

"He loves the place so much, and he was so hurt when Sir Antony sent him away. I told you how he lived here and did your job. He seemed so happy to be back that I thought he might like to stay for a little while."

"Well, now, we could manage," Ann said thoughtfully. "He'd keep out o' sight when people came, I suppose?"

"Oh, yes! He'd understand that. He has friends in the village. He knows the Spindles, at the forge. He'd go to them during the day. But he'd like to feel he was living in the Abbey. He can afford to pay you for his meals—you'd arrange that with him—he has a small pension. It's the idea of living in the Abbey again that I want to give him."

"Sort of to comfort him, like, the poor old chap." Ann responded to the appeal with unexpected understanding. "I'll do it, Miss Joan. I'll make him comfortable."

Joan thanked her quietly and went away, bidding her explain to Mr. Browning when he woke. "So that's that!" she said to herself, as she crossed the garth. "It was better to say it was only for a few days. We'll see how he likes the idea, and how they get on together. I didn't think Ann would be so nice about it. But I believe she's beginning to love the Abbey, so perhaps she feels sorry for him. I hope she will love the place. If she does, she may settle down and stay for years. I hope she will. I don't want to have constant changes, and Ann does the job very well. Jenny-Wren?"

Jen's head appeared at a window. "Joan! You've been to the Abbey without me! You rotter!"

"Not at all. You were sound asleep. Come down, and I'll tell you why I went so early."

Jen came flying out to join her. "Breakfast on the terrace, in the sun! Oh, please, Joan! I'll help to carry! You put up the table; I'll bring chairs."

"Quickly, then." And Joan set up the folding table and piled breakfast dishes on a tray.

"There!" Jen said, with much satisfaction. "I love outdoor breakfasts. Everything smells so fresh. Oh, Joan! Is Boniface all right? Did you go to see him?"

"I didn't see him. He was still asleep. I went to speak to Ann. She talked to him last night, and she likes him; she says he seems a nice, quiet old gentleman, but she's bothered about his asthma."

"That sounds as if she'd like to take care of him. Oh, if only——!"

"If only what, Jen?"

"If only she had another room! If we could

make a room for him somewhere! Ann could be the head of the infirmary for the aged poor, as well as the caretaker for the Abbey. He can't have your room, of course, but if there was somewhere else——!"

"I've told Ann she may invite him to stay for a few days," Joan said. "It seemed better—— what's the matter, you silly kid?"

Jen, with a shriek of joy, had started up and rushed round the table to hug her ecstatically. "Oh, Joan! How marvellous! You're an absolute angel! Don't you mind?"

"You very nearly upset the table; it's not too steady. Stop strangling me, or I won't tell you any more!"

Jen released her hurriedly. "Tell me! Will Ann look after him? Perhaps she'll like him so much that she won't want him to go away!"

"It seemed better to say 'a few days' at first," Joan went on, straightening the cloth and the dishes. "We'll see how Boniface likes the idea and how Ann and he get on together. I didn't want to frighten her by suggesting he should live there altogether."

"But if they're both pleased, would you let him stay?" Jen asked breathlessly, eyeing her in rapture. "Oh, Joan, would you? But it's your room! You couldn't give it up, even for Boniface Browning! Joan, what do you mean?"

"I feel that the Abbey customs must be upheld, when a chance comes," Joan explained soberly.

"Here is an old man, who loves the Abbey and quite obviously wants to stay. The monks wouldn't have turned him away. I can make him welcome by giving up my room. He'll do no harm and be no trouble to anyone. I haven't any choice. It's an Abbey duty, and the Abbey is mine. Don't you agree?"

"Of *course* I do! But it's awfully, frightfully decent of you to see it that way." Jen, gazing wide-eyed, surprised Joan by taking the idea very quietly, instead of with one of her well-known shrieks of joy. The same thing had happened when she had invited Jen to be her maid-of-honour in the May Day procession. The occasion, it seemed, was too great for a joyful shout, and Jen's next words, spoken quietly, confirmed this.

"It makes the Abbey seem so real," she said.

"How do you mean, Jen? The Abbey is real enough."

"The buildings are real, but the ideas behind them—the monks and their good deeds, and all that—seem sometimes a bit dream-like. It was so very long ago! But when you do something like this—giving up your own precious room, so that the Abbey can welcome an aged and infirm person who loves it—then the monks and the Abbot, and Ambrose and Jehane, all seem quite real. You're bringing back the ancient custom, because the Abbey is yours. It's simply marvellous!"

Joan coloured at the deep feeling in her tone.

"I don't see what else I could do. I want old Boniface to be happy."

"But you want to keep your room, don't you?"

"I want both. If Boniface wants to stay—we don't know yet that he does—I may as well choose the way that will please both of us."

"And me! It makes me terribly happy, to think he'll have the chance to end his days in the Abbey."

"I haven't suggested that yet. I've only invited him to stay for a few days."

Jen nodded. "But you won't send him away, if he likes being here. You're a real descendant of the monks."

"I've never claimed to be that! I'm not nearly as generous as you think. If Boniface feels he must go back to his son in Birmingham, I shall be overjoyed. But I do feel he has to be given the chance to stay."

"Because the monks would have kept him," Jen agreed. "Will you mind very much if he decides to stay?"

"I shall miss my little room," Joan said honestly. "But he'll need to have it, for there's nowhere else. I shall leave him to think it over. Ann will tell him what I said. You and I have something to do to-day."

Jen looked up quickly. "I'd forgotten about Vinny Miles. And—oh, Joan, the tree! I'd forgotten it too. They're going to murder it to-day. Oh, Joan!"

"It's better to think about giving a happy old

age to Boniface than about a tree which has begun
to die," Joan said practically. "We'll go at once,
and we won't go through the Abbey. I want the
old chap to think over the idea before I speak to
him. Fetch your jersey, Jen. We'll take the short-
cut to the village, across the fields."

"Across the great church," Jen agreed. "We
know now what it used to look like."

"Yes, thanks to you and Jacky-boy and Sir Keith
Marchwood. Come along!"

CHAPTER VII

VINNY NOT AT HOME

JEN kept her face resolutely turned from the ruins as they crossed the site of the great church, and Joan rejoiced to see it. But at the wicket-gate by which they went out into the fields she looked back and, with a catch in her breath, waved her hand to the giant elm which hung over the gate-house. Then she ran down the path, and Joan ran after her. "We'll see if the village can find us a red ribbon for Lavinia, Jen."

"Yes—oh, yes! It will save a lot of time if we don't have to go all the way to Wycombe." Jen sounded a trifle breathless and incoherent, but her voice grew steadier as she spoke. "I wonder if we'll see Vinny at the farm? I expect Mrs. Jaikes makes her work in the house during the holidays."

"We mustn't be too late, for Jandy comes to-day," Joan reminded her.

"Yes. It will be fun to have Jandy Mac all to ourselves. We must tell her about these new people—Lavinia and dear old Boniface."

The village was able to supply red ribbon, to Jen's delight. Urged on by Joan, she chose a length of crimson. "That's the right colour, not bright scarlet," she said, "though I don't suppose Lavinia would care if we made her wear scarlet with a crimson dress! She'll love it. We'll take enough for two big bows, and make her wear her hair in two bunches; she's got rather a lot."

It was not a long walk to King's Bottom Farm, which stood at the entrance to one of the combes running up into the hills. Joan made the walk longer, however, by proposing to go up over the green shoulder of hill and drop down to the farm from above. She had her own reasons for insisting on the extra tramp; Jen must not return to the Abbey too soon.

They stood in the wind on the crest of the hill and looked northwards to the Whiteleaf Cross and west to Thame and the distant blue country. The Abbey and the Hall, the Manor and the village, lay almost at their feet, and closer still, right below, was King's Bottom Farm.

"Come on!" Joan said. "Now for Lavinia and Mrs. Jaikes!"

"Vinny?" The tall thin woman at the farmhouse door sounded indignant. "Drat the child! I dunno where she is. Run off and left me all on my own, she has, and knowin' well enough I've more to do than I can get through. At least she could mind the kids! I can't do nothing with Vinny, some days."

"I'm sorry she isn't here. She ought to help," Joan agreed. "Perhaps we'll meet her on our way home. Mrs. Jaikes, Jen Robins—this is Jen—was talking to Lavinia yesterday, and Vinny told her about her relations in America. We know you've been very kind, keeping her since her aunt died, but don't you think she really ought to be with her own people? Her father is still alive, isn't he?"

"Aye, but there's a stepmother. Sometimes they don't want a man's first family. Sure, I think she did ought to go to them, and I'd be glad to see the back of her. But how could she go, a bit of a thing like her?"

"Perhaps they could come to fetch her," Jen put in, eager to help.

"Costs too much," Mrs. Jaikes said briefly. "And we can't send her. Jaikes and me has as much as we can do with our own. 'Sides, 'tisn't only the money. Who'd take care of the kid on the journey?"

"It is difficult," Joan agreed. "But you do think she ought to go, Mrs. Jaikes?"

"I do. Her own folks had oughter have the care of her. She's got folks. They'd oughter keep her. We didn't oughter have to do it."

"No, it's hard on you. I'm sure you've been very good. Have you her father's address?"

"I got it somewheres. I been a-thinking I'd oughter write to him, but—well, I'm no great hand with a pen, and Jaikes, he's worse."

"If you could find the address, we would write the letter for you," Joan suggested. "We'd remind Vinny's father that she's quite a big girl now, and ask if he couldn't think of some way to get her back to her family."

Mrs. Jaikes looked at her doubtfully. "You'll say as how I done my best for Vinny, and no pay for doing it? If he's doing well out there, he'd oughter make it up to me. I'd thought that was what I'd say, if I wrote."

"Yes, we'd say that," Joan promised. "But I expect Vinny has been a great help to you with your babies, although she has run away to-day."

"She ain't done very much—not near as much as I'd have liked," Mrs. Jaikes said. "I'll have a look for the address. I got it somewheres. If I find it I'll make Vinny bring it along to you."

"Yes, please do. We'll look out for her on our way home." And Joan turned to go, followed by a silent Jen.

"You didn't leave the ribbon for Lavinia, Joan?"

"Don't you want to give it to her yourself? I thought it was better not to give it to Mrs. Jaikes."

"She might have bagged it for her own infants," Jen admitted. "I don't like the creature, do you?"

"Not very much. But one can sympathise with her. She's had Lavinia left on her hands, and she's done her best for her, and then Vinny runs away and leaves her with the children and the house-work to do all alone. It isn't fair."

"No, Vinny isn't being sporting," Jen owned. "But I expect she's completely fed up. She sounded like it."

"It would be easier to help her, if she played the game. She gives Mrs. Jaikes a real grievance. I shall scold Lavinia," Joan said decidedly.

"Don't make her more fed up than she is already!" Jen pleaded hurriedly. "She thinks such a lot of you!"

"I'll be careful," Joan promised, much amused. "Now, Jen, we can't go home yet; it's too soon. What shall we do with ourselves?"

Their eyes met in complete understanding. "Whatever you like, Joan-Queen," Jen said gloomily.

"Then come with me!" And Joan set her face to the hills again. "We'll go to Wycombe, after all, and have a spot of lunch, and then we'll come home by bus to the village."

"We shan't meet Lavinia, if we go that way."

"We might. She may be up on the hills. Keep a look-out for her."

"I expect she's gone to the Abbey, to say good-bye to our poor tree again."

"That won't make her feel any better. It's a pity she didn't stay at home and keep herself busy by helping Mrs. Jaikes."

"Perhaps she'll meet old Boniface," Jen remarked.

"She may know him. It's only three years since he left the Abbey," Joan reminded her. "But she may never have gone there in his day. I don't suppose he encouraged the village kiddies to hang about."

"I think Lavinia only went there to see you, when you had your drill class."

"That's quite possible," Joan assented.

"What did you do with them? I'd like to see you being a teacher!"

"Oh, marching and wand drill, and free-arm exercises. There were some green stakes the gardener used, and we helped ourselves to those. I was very fierce and made them keep strict time to my counting, if Joy was out and we couldn't have music."

"We'll write to Joy. There's a lot to tell her— Lavinia and Boniface, you know."

"I shall write to Mother to-morrow; they'll be wanting letters. You can write to Joy."

"And Jandy Mac can write to her Alec. So we'll all be busy. We'll buy a present for Boniface in Wycombe." Jen cheered up at the thought. "If we take red ribbon for Lavinia, we must take something for him too. What would he like, do you think?"

"Tobacco, I expect," Joan said, with a laugh. "But we wouldn't know what sort to buy."

"The man in the shop would tell us. Or what about sweets? Don't old people like sweets?"

"I'm sure they do. Sweets would be best. We'll find something for Boniface," Joan promised.

"Something better than he could get in the village! There's much more choice in Wycombe." And Jen looked happier as they climbed the hill.

CHAPTER VIII

THE TREE FALLS

As JOAN said later, things happened all at once.

With Jen, she walked up the lane from the village, and stopped in dismay as they reached the Abbey gate, for the big tree was still standing, though shorn of its branches. Matthew Edwards had promised to have the work finished in good time, but the men were still busy, with ropes round the great trunk to control its fall.

"I didn't trust Mr. Edwards. I was afraid he'd be late," Joan groaned. "We'll go on and up the avenue, Jen."

Jen's lips were quivering as she looked at the tree. "No," she said bravely. "It's much farther, and you're tired. We'll go through the Abbey. We won't look. Oh, Joan, there's Lavinia! Do you see her red frock? I said she'd come to watch. There, by the gate-house, in the corner!"

"Silly child!" Joan said indignantly. "Has she been watching them saw off the branches? What a senseless thing to do!"

Jen stood looking past the tree, which swayed, ready to fall. "There's old Boniface, by the Abbey door. He's just come out. He wants to see—oh! Oh, I say! She'll be right under the tree!"

A flash of red—Vinny Miles had darted towards

the old man, with a shout which sounded like "Uncle Bonny!"

A streak of blue—Jen was after her, just as the tree crashed to the ground.

"Jen! Jen!" Joan shrieked. "Oh, Jen! Why did you do it?"

Shaking with fear, she rushed with the men to the tree, which lay stretched on the meadow. The two small girls were underneath.

"We'll get them out, Miss Joan," panted one of the men. "Maybe they aren't much hurt."

"They came so quick," groaned another. "We couldn't do nothing."

"We was all running to stop that there Vinny Miles, but little miss was faster than any of us," said the first, as they wrestled with the mass of small branches which had fallen with the tree.

"Oh, be quick!" Joan sobbed. "Get them out! Help me!" And she struggled to lift the boughs.

"We'll do it, miss." The men were working in feverish haste.

"Here's Vinny. Her be all right. Little missy flung her forward and then fell a-top of her."

Joan looked round wildly, for Jen still lay buried.

"Mr. Browning, call Ann Watson and ask her to see to Vinny," she cried to the old man, who had come hurrying up. "I can't think about her just now. She isn't much hurt." For Vinny, white with terror, was asking weakly what had happened.

Joan turned from her to the men, who had prised up a short bough which was pinning Jen down. They drew her out very gently and began to examine her limp body with careful hands.

"I dunno," said one. "Best get her to the house and send for doctor."

"She isn't—isn't——" Joan began brokenly.

"Her's not dead. Heart's all right. But it hit her head," said one of the men. "Look! It caught her there. Didn't touch her back; that's one good thing."

"I thought her back would be broke," growled somebody.

"Dry up, you fool!" snapped another. "It's her head, not her back. She'll come round soon. But best have doctor."

"Put her on this. Lift her gentle like." Two lads, with great presence of mind, had rushed to the farm and brought a hurdle.

Feeling dazed and numb, Joan followed, as Jen was carried carefully through the Abbey door and across the garth. It had all happened so suddenly. Five minutes ago they had been walking up from the village. Now Jenny-Wren might be dying— for these men did not know very much.

She unlocked the gate, and they went through the garden.

"If you'd run on and ring up doctor, Miss Joan," a man began.

Joan pulled herself together. "Yes. Thank you

—yes, I'll go. But don't touch her. We don't know what's wrong. She may be hurt—injured——"

She caught her breath in a sob and ran to the house, thankful as she had seldom been that Joy had insisted on having the telephone put in as soon as the Hall came into her hands.

Then, with the promise that the doctor would come at once, she went to help. "Leave her lying just as she is," she ordered. "The doctor will be here in a few minutes. He'll know if it's safe to move her." She brought rugs and spread them over Jen, who lay still and unconscious.

"Perhaps two of you would wait, in case he wants her carried upstairs on the hurdle," Joan suggested unsteadily.

The men withdrew to the terrace, silent and unhappy, and Joan dropped into a chair, her eyes on Jen.

"The worst few minutes of my life," she said afterwards.

Then, with a quick, silent leap, she was beside the stretcher, for Jen's eyes had opened.

"Joan?" she whispered drowsily. Then, more clearly: "Oh, Joan! Vinny! Was I in time? Did the tree hurt her?"

"Oh, thank God!" Joan whispered, and dropped on her knees because they were shaking so terribly. "It's all right, Jen, dear. You saved Vinny. She isn't hurt. You pushed her out of the way."

"Oh, good! I thought she'd be killed," Jen

murmured. "Did it hit me, too? I'm so tired, Joan-Queen!"

"Try to go to sleep," Joan urged unsteadily. "The doctor's coming to have a look at you, just to see if any parts of you are broken. Does anything hurt you, Jen?"

"I feel sore all over. I'd like to go to bed. But I can kick and I can hold your hand." And Jen demonstrated by a feeble kick of each leg in turn and by gripping Joan's eager hands. "I don't think anything's broken."

"I'm sure nothing's broken. You'll be all right, Jenny-Wren. But we'll wait for the doctor to make certain. Hold my hand and lie still."

"I shall go to sleep," Jen said wearily.

There was great thankfulness in Joan's heart as she crouched on the floor, holding Jen's hand. "She can't be badly hurt. She can't! If there was concussion, it's passing off. Here's the doctor. He's been very quick,"—at the sound of the men, speaking to someone on the terrace.

Then she looked up in startled unbelief, as words reached her, spoken in a clear, girl's voice.

"Not go in? Of course, I shall go in! What's wrong with you all?"

"Jandy!" Joan whispered. "Hours earlier than we expected!"

She tried to draw away her hand, but Jen's grip tightened at once. Helpless, Joan knelt on, but looked up at Janice as she came in.

"Why are you being a tableau? Is it charades?" Janice cried gaily.

"Don't, Jandy! Don't wake her. We're waiting for the doctor," Joan faltered.

"Oh—Joan! Oh, my dear, I'm so sorry! What has happened?" Janice tiptoed to her. "Is she hurt? Oh, Joan, what's the matter?"

"I can't get up. She's clinging to my hand. We daren't move her till the doctor has examined her. But I think she's all right," Joan said, very quietly. "She spoke to me and she was quite sensible."

"Sensible!" Jen's eyes were suddenly wide open. "I should hope so! Did you think I'd been knocked silly? Hallo, Jandy Mac! What are you doing here? You weren't coming till the evening!"

Janice dropped limply into a chair. "I thought you were dead!"

"Well, you needn't, for I'm not." But Jen's voice was very weak and tired. "I'm all right, but the big tree came down and hit me. How did you get here so soon, Jandy Mac?"

Janice looked at Joan. "May she talk?"

"I'd rather she didn't. Tell her why you're so early. I thought you were only to reach London about six?"

"I travelled by night and spent a few hours in town. Alec asked me to see some people for him. I walked up from the station. My bag's there, waiting to be collected. Why don't you have taxis?"

"Here's the doctor!" Joan said quickly, at the sound of a car. "Run upstairs, Jandy, there's a dear! Your old room is ready. I'll come and tell you all about it presently."

Janice turned to the staircase. "Good luck, Jenny-Wren!" she said gently. "Sorry I butted in. I'll be waiting for you, Joan, dear. Come as soon as you can. You look all done in. I shall have to take care of you both, I think."

CHAPTER IX

JEN REMEMBERS

JANICE MACDONALD, a pretty dark girl with wavy brown hair cut short, was stowing away the things she had brought from the station in her small case, when Joan came quietly in.

"It's all right, Jandy Mac. The doctor has put Jen to bed, and he says we're not to worry. I'll tell you how it happened, but there's a lot I don't understand myself." She dropped wearily into a chair by the window. "Jen will be all right; that's the big thing. She's badly bruised and she has a big lump on the back of her head, but nothing is broken. She'll need to rest for a few days and be kept quiet—if anyone can keep Jen quiet! But there's nothing to be worried about. Oh, Jandy Mac! I had the fright of my life when I thought she was dead!"

"You poor thing! I'm sure you did. I could see what a shock you had had," Janice said gently. "I suppose that tree by the gate-house hit her when it fell? I saw it as I came up the lane. But why was Jen in the way? What was she doing near the tree?"

"She's been interested in a village child called Lavinia, or Vinny. Vinny loved that tree, and she was there, watching the men take it down——"

"One thing!" Janice begged. "Why were they doing it? Why did you allow it?"

"It was diseased; it had to come down. We felt terrible about it, but there was no other way. Jen was heart-broken. I've kept her out on the hills all day, hoping it would be over before we came home. But the men hadn't finished, and the tree was just coming down as we came back. Young Vinny was watching, and suddenly she rushed out right under the tree, and we all thought she'd be killed. That's the part I don't understand. I can't think why she did such a mad thing."

"And Jen tried to stop her?"

"Jen rushed after her and flung her almost clear. They were caught by the small branches that hadn't been lopped off, and Jen got the worst of it. I thought her back might be broken." And Joan shivered, looking white.

Janice glanced at her anxiously. "You weren't fit for such a shock. Try not to think about it, Joan, dear. Remember that it hasn't happened. You said Jen would be all right. Stick to that! Say it over and over again: 'Jenny-Wren's all right!' We can't let you have nightmares and go off your sleep. And you must think what a little brick Jen was. Fancy running into such danger to save the child!"

"Running! She went like a flash. I never saw her go so quickly. The men all ran, but she was far ahead of everybody."

"Did she realise the danger?" Janice asked curiously.

"I think she did. She called out, 'She'll be right under the tree!' and rushed to the rescue."

"Plucky kid! I've always loved Jenny-Wren. This isn't the first time she has been brave."

"In those tunnels," Joan agreed, looking out of the window, where the men were carrying the hurdle across the lawn. "I must thank the boys who thought of bringing that thing. It was just what was needed. I expect they're Scouts. I asked them to take it away and to hurry on with the business. I want all signs of that tree cleared up as soon as possible; I've had more than enough of it."

Janice assented. "It must go now. It would always remind you of Jen and the other child."

"Lavinia. I must see if she's all right. But she wasn't hurt; I heard her asking what had happened. I forgot all about her—I was so frightened for Jen. I think I said Mrs. Watson must look after her."

"I'll come with you and we'll ask what she meant by running out like that. But couldn't we have some tea first?" Janice looked anxiously at Joan's strained face. "I want my tea, Joan. I had a hot tramp from the station."

"Yes, of course. Tea is the first thing. It will be ready ; let's go down. Oh, Jandy, I am so glad you're here! It's a real comfort to have you for company!"

"I'm glad I'm here," Janice said sturdily. "You need somebody to look after you. It's too soon after your illness for you to have shocks like this."

"I wasn't really ill, you know. But we had a very bad time with Joy; we thought we were going to lose her for a day or two. I'm thankful she and Mother are away. This business would have been bad for them both."

"How are they? I was terribly sorry to hear of Mrs. Shirley's breakdown."

"Poor Mother just collapsed when Joy was so ill; it was too much for her. They're better, and the holiday will do them all the good in the world. But Mother ought not to have any more shocks, I shan't tell her about Jen till she comes home."

"Much better not. What about Jen's own people?"

"There's no need to worry them, since she isn't in any danger. She'll be going home in a few days, and she can tell them the story herself."

"I'm sorry I spoilt your holiday," Janice said, as they sat down to tea.

"I didn't really want to go and live in an hotel. I'd rather be at home. Tell me about your journey! Did you sleep? Aren't you terribly tired?"

"Not a scrap. I slept well, and I was quite fresh this morning."

Janice was still talking of her Scottish aunts and of boating on the wild, beautiful loch and roaming on the hills, and trying to take Joan's thoughts off the disasters of the day, when a tiny maid knocked and entered.

"Please, Miss Joan, would you come and speak to Miss Jen?"

"It's Susie Spindle. I told you her story in my letters," Joan said in a low voice. "I left her sitting with Jen. I'll come, Susie. But why isn't Jen asleep? You haven't been talking to her, have you?"

"Not more as I couldn't help, Miss Joan. But Miss Jen, she kept thinking of things."

"Very hard on Susie," Janice remarked. "We know Jen! You'd better go and see what's on her mind, Joan. May I come too?"

"She knows you're here, but perhaps she thinks she dreamt about you. Come and show her you're real!" And they bent together over Jen's bed.

"What's the matter, Jen? You bad girl! You're supposed to be asleep," Joan scolded gently.

Jen's eyes went from one to the other. "Jolly good thing Jandy Mac's here to be company for you! I've let you down badly, haven't I? Oh, Joan, I remembered something! I've been to sleep and I'm going again, but I woke up remembering. Susie doesn't know anything about it, so I had to have you. Joan, when Vinny ran under that tree, did you hear what she said?"

"I know she called out something, but I didn't hear the words. But it can wait, Jen. I want you to stop thinking about the tree."

"I'm going to stop. I'm tired, and I'm going

to sleep. But I want you to find Vinny and ask her what she meant."

"Then I shall have to do it, I suppose. What did Vinny say?"

"She saw old Boniface at the Abbey door, and she yelled, ' Uncle Bonny! ' He couldn't really be her uncle, Joan!"

"I'll tell you about Boniface presently, Jandy Mac," Joan said. "No, Jen, he couldn't be her uncle; he's far too old. But she may have known him when he lived in the Abbey. Perhaps all the children called him Uncle Bonny."

"Go and ask her!" Jen pleaded. "I want to know. It would be fun if he was her real, proper uncle, and it would be awfully convenient. He could take care of her. Perhaps he could take her to America!"

"Jenny-Wren, you're altogether too bright and sparkling for an invalid!" Joan said reproachfully.

"It sounds like a nightmare," Janice remarked. "Have you been dreaming, Jenny-Wren? What's all this about America and somebody called something very odd?"

"Good old Boniface!" Jen murmured. "Go and ask Vinny, Joan. Or if they've sent her home, ask him. He'll know if he's her uncle."

"He's too old to be Lavinia's uncle," Joan said again. "But I want to know if she's all right, so I'll ask what he thinks she meant, at the same time. I shan't tell you any more about it until to-morrow, so the sooner you forget it all and go to sleep, the sooner you'll hear what Boniface Browning says."

"Yes, Joan, dear," Jen said submissively. "So long as you're finding out, I can bear to wait. But I had to tell you Vinny said he was her uncle. I didn't think you'd heard."

"I was too much upset about you to hear anything," Joan retorted. "How do you think I felt when you charged out, right under that tree?"

Jen glanced up at her and saw in her eyes something of what that moment had been.

"Sorry!" she murmured. "But I thought the kid would be squashed flat. I had to try to get her out."

"Go to sleep!" Joan commanded, and bent and kissed her.

"Take care of Joan, Jandy Mac!" was Jen's last word.

"'Squashed flat'!" Joan shuddered when she and Janice were safely downstairs again. "Just what I thought too, but not about Vinny Miles!"

"Don't think about it! What's this talk of America? And who is the very old person with the weird name?"

"Boniface Browning. It really is his name! He was the caretaker in the Abbey till he grew too old. When he was sent away, Mother and I took over. He turned up last night, when Jen and I were having a midnight picnic in the Abbey."

"Joan! Is that what happens when your mother goes away?" Janice cried.

"It wasn't really midnight; more like nine or ten o'clock. Jen begged for it, to celebrate our one night alone together, and I couldn't refuse her."

"Wish I'd been here, instead of in the train! You might have waited for me!"

"Jen went wandering about by moonlight, while I packed the picnic stuff. Suddenly she came flying back, terrified, screaming that she had seen old Ambrose in the sacristy. She doesn't believe in ghosts, and yet she had seen a very old man with a long white beard. She'd had a real shock. I knew him as soon as I saw him. He came out to apologise." And Joan told how Mr. Browning had stayed behind the other tourists, because of his love for the Abbey, and of Jen's idea that he should be invited to end his days there and so bring back the ancient custom of tending aged and infirm folk.

She explained her invitation to Mr. Browning, and Janice pursed her lips. "To live in your private room? But you won't be able to use it any more?"

"No, I shall have to give it up to Boniface—as Jen calls him all the time. There's no other place for him."

"I don't approve," Janice said hotly. "It's your one little spot. Why should you give it up? The old chap has a home of his own."

"We don't know yet that he'll want to stay here. He may choose to go back to Birmingham," Joan said hopefully.

"Don't you think it! If he's keen on your Abbey, he'll like it much better than a city. You'll have him on your hands till he dies."

"That's Jenny-Wren's idea. The monks used to do it, and she wants me to revive the custom."

"Will you like knowing this old man is always there, quite apart from giving up your room?" Janice demanded. "You've felt that once the gate was closed to tourists, the Abbey belonged to you. Now old Browning will be there, wandering about all over the place. Do you like the thought of it?"

"No," Joan admitted. "I shall lose my Abbey. I shan't go there as I used to do. I feel rather bad about it. But I couldn't disappoint Jen, Jandy!"

Janice frowned. "It isn't sensible, Joan. I know you're a saint and an angel and the right person to have charge of the Abbey, but this is doing too much. You'll spoil the place for yourself and for everybody, if you have an old man about all the time."

"Ass!" said Joan indignantly. "I'm so little of a saint and angel that I'm hoping desperately Boniface won't want to stay, or his son won't agree. He's an old dear; they may insist on keeping him in Birmingham. Or he and Ann Watson may not get on well together—that's very important!"

"But if none of those hoped-for things happens, you'll give in and keep him here?"

"I feel," Joan explained, "that the monks have

asked me to give Boniface the chance. I can't let the Abbey down."

Janice shrugged her shoulders. "It's too much to do for an idea out of the past."

"Perhaps it is. But I have to do it."

Janice softened towards her suddenly. "You are a jolly decent old thing! I won't scold any more. I hope your Abbey won't be spoiled for you, that's all."

"It might be spoiled, if I refused," Joan said quietly. "As I've had the idea, I'd never feel quite comfortable in there again if I'd turned Boniface down."

"No, he'd haunt you," Janice agreed. "Let's go and tackle him! Perhaps he'll say he can only stay for a day or two."

Joan's face lit up. "That would be an easy way out. Come and ask him if he really is anybody's uncle, Jandy Mac!"

CHAPTER X

UNCLE BONNY

"MR. BROWNING would like to speak to you, Miss Joan." Susie Spindle met the girls as they went downstairs.

"Is he here?" Joan exclaimed. "Bring him into the library, Susie. We were going to the Abbey to look for him."

"He'd do very well for Ambrose," Janice murmured, as the old man appeared in the doorway. "I really don't blame Jenny-Wren. If I'd seen him first by moonlight, not knowing there was anybody in the Abbey, I'd have yelled myself. He might quite well be the ghost of Ambrose!"

"Is little Lavinia all right, Boniface?" Joan asked. "I said something about asking Mrs. Watson to look after her, didn't I? It was such a muddle for a moment, that I hardly know what happened."

"Her be well enough, Miss Joan. I done what you says and called Mrs. Watson. Vinny were only frit; her hadn't took no hurt. Us sent her home to farm."

Jandy's eyes met Joan's, full of laughter. Later, Joan remarked that she hoped Mr. Browning's conversation had grown worse since he gave up his job at the Abbey.

But he was very much in earnest, and he hurried on.

"I thanks ye, Miss Joan, for that kind thought o' yourn. I'd be mighty pleased to bide in the old place for a few days. Like home, it seems to me. I'll never feel settled-like in a town. My son be good to me, but they've a pack o' youngsters, and they haven't much room. Always kids about all the time. I likes 'em well enough, but I'm old now, and the noise and clatter frets me. 'Tis quiet in the Abbey, and it be like home to come back. It's real kind of ye to think o' me."

"You must stay for a while and have a good rest," Joan said quietly.

"'Deed I will, if you'll put up wi' me, miss, and I thanks ye more than I can say. Is the other little lass badly hurt, Miss Joan? She were sweet to me last night, giving me cushions an' makin' me easy-like. The men did say as how she might have broke her back. I hope it isn't so?"

"She might have done, but she didn't. It must have been only a small branch that knocked her down. She has to rest for a few days, and she has some bad bruises, but nothing's broken, I'm thankful to say."

"Glory be! I were afeared for the lass. I'll tell Mrs. Watson. She were frit about her too. When I saw that small maid run right under the tree, my heart, it just stopped, Miss Joan."

"So did mine," Joan assured him. "But there's

no need to worry any more. She'll be all right in a day or two."

"It's glad I be to hear it. I spoke very rough to Vinny and told her she were to blame, and if little Miss Jen died, it were her had done it."

"Poor Vinny! Boniface, Jen says that when Lavinia ran to you she called you ' Uncle Bonny '. You aren't really her uncle, are you?"

"I were uncle to her mother, what died years ago, Miss Joan. Vinny's always called me Uncle Bonny."

"Oh, I see! Her great-uncle. How odd! I didn't know she was related to you."

"Lizzie Miles, her mother was. But her first name were Lizzie Browning. My brother's girl, Lizzie was. But she died, and her man, that was Vinny's dad, went off to 'Mercy with the boys and left Vinny with Mary Ann, that was Lizzie's sister, and then she died too, Miss Joan."

"This is getting complicated!" Joan exclaimed. "Your brother had two girls, Lizzie and Mary Ann. Lizzie was Vinny's mother, Mrs. Miles. Mary Ann was the aunt who stayed at the farm when the family went to America—the one who took care of Vinny and then died. Is that right?"

"That be the way of it, Miss Joan. I were uncle to Liz and Mary Ann, but they be both gone now."

"So now you are uncle to Lavinia. Perhaps you could advise us," Joan said thoughtfully. "We want to help her, but we thought she had nobody of her own left in this country. Since she has you, we must certainly consult you. But not to-night; I must talk it over with Jen first."

"I'd like to help the lass. Her's not too happy at the farm, now Mary Ann's gone. But what to do for her I do not know, Miss Joan. I thanks ye for thinkin' of the child, and for bein' so kind to me, sayin' as how I may bide in the Abbey for a day or two. I'll tell my son, and I'll fetch my bits o' things from Spindles'."

"How do you like Mrs. Watson, Boniface?"

"Her be a very pleasant lady, and very kind. Her give me a wonnerful breakfast 'smorning, and her were gentle with Vinny, when the lass were crying her eyes out along of little Miss Jen being hurt. We told Vinny Miss Jen looked just like death when the lads carried her off, and Vinny knew 'twas her fault and her cried and cried."

"Poor Vinny! That was too bad," Joan exclaimed. "I must send a message, to tell her Jen will be all right. I'm glad Mrs. Watson was kind to her. Boniface!"—and she braced herself for a great effort. "Would you like to come and live in the Abbey? To stay there altogether, I mean? Not just for a few days?"

Boniface stared at her, his eyes widening, his face lighting up in incredulous joy. "Oh, Miss Joan! Do ye mean I'd make my home there and bide there to end my days?"

"I wouldn't have put it that way," Joan said gently. "But I do mean that. You love the

Abbey, and it's peaceful and quiet, with no noisy children. We could only give you that one tiny room, and you'd have to keep out of the way during tourist times. But you could spend the day in the village or at one of the farms, and the Abbey would be your home. Mrs. Watson would give you your meals. You'd pay her something each week for your food, but not for the room, of course."

"For her trouble," Boniface murmured, looking dazed. "It would mean all the world to me, to end my days here. The many times I've thought about the Abbey, away there in the city! I've wanted it so much that I just had to come back to see it all once more. Oh, Miss Joan, you couldn't of meant that, surely! I haven't a lot of stuff; I'd fit into the small room nicely. I'd sooner be here than anywheres in the world! Well, no, I wouldn't say that. There's one other place I'd sooner go. But that can't be, so it's no use to think o't."

"Where is the other place?" Joan asked curiously.

"Nay, 'tain't possible, not for an old 'un like me. I'll not think or talk of it."

"But tell me, Boniface! I'd like to know."

"Some day, maybe, but not now. I thought of it once, but I'm past it. But if I could bide in the Abbey I'd be happy. I never dreamt of anything so good, Miss Joan. May I ask Mrs. Watson if she'd do for me?"

"Ask her if she'd be willing to take care of

you," Joan agreed. "That's very important. She has her work in the Abbey. We mustn't ask too much of her."

"I could be of use to her," the old man said, tremulous with eagerness. "It were the stairs that was too much for me. I could mind the gate while she showed folks round, and I could do a bit o' dusting, to help her. I knows all there is to do. And I could fetch her bits of shopping from village. I'd do anything to be useful, Miss Joan."

"Go and talk it over with her," Joan advised. "And you must write to your son. He may not want to lose you."

"They'll be glad to have my room," Boniface said, rather desolately. "They been kind, but they ain't got the place for me. They only took me in because I hadn't nowheres else to go. It near broke my heart to leave the Abbey, Miss Joan."

"I guessed that." Joan's eyes were kind. "I felt you would like to come back."

"I never could of dreamed of anything so good," Boniface said earnestly.

"Then go and talk it over with Mrs. Watson. Tell her I'll see her in the morning. And tell her Jen will be all right, Boniface."

"I do thank ye, Miss Joan." The old man still looked dazed with happiness, as he followed Joan to the door and went off across the lawn to the Abbey gate.

"You've done it now, Joan, girl," Janice said

severely, when Joan returned. "You've burnt your boats. You can't go back on it now."

"I felt I must do it, so that I couldn't draw back," Joan admitted. "But once I'd said it, I didn't want to withdraw. Did you ever see anybody look more radiantly happy?"

"Oh, he's perfectly enraptured, of course! It's the great event of his life. You'll never get rid of him! And he'll live for years and years in the peace of the Abbey. How old is he? He'll be on your hands till he's ninety-five!"

"I believe he's seventy-three. Sir Antony thought he ought to retire at seventy, and you can't blame him. Boniface couldn't do the job now."

"You'll have him here for twenty years."

Joan flinched a little. "Perhaps not. But I hope he'll have a few happy years. I can't be sorry, when I remember the look on his face. Even if it keeps me from coming into the Abbey so much, it's worth it to have made Boniface look like that! And Jen is right; the Abbey will be doing its proper work again, giving shelter to someone who needs it. It's a very satisfying thought."

"Will it comfort you for losing the Abbey for yourself?"

"I may not lose it," Joan retorted. "I can't pretend that I like the thought of there being someone always there, but Boniface is an old dear. He may not be so much in the way as I think. He'll keep out of sight when I'm there."

"Not he! He'll want to come and talk and thank you for being so kind."

"I'll explain that I want to be quiet. He loves the Abbey so much that he'll understand. I wonder what he meant about some other place where he would rather be?"

"He was very mysterious about it. He'll tell you some day. He's going to worship the ground you tread on."

"Ass!" Joan said. "Jandy, I must write to that poor kid Lavinia."

"They've frightened her badly, among them," Janice agreed.

"Yes, they've terrified her. She must be told Jen is all right, or she'll cry herself sick. I really can't go all the way to the farm again! We were there this morning. But she must be reassured to-night. I shall send a note. I'll find some boy to take it."

"Send Boniface. Make him useful!"

"No, he's too old. But there are boys about the farm. Susie will find one. She knows them all."

"Could somebody fetch my baggage from the station? I'm sorry to be a nuisance, but I really couldn't lug it up through the woods."

"Of course not. I'll send for it. Joy has taken the car, but there's a carrier in the village. I'll ring him up, and the station."

"Thanks, old dear. Then I'll go and write to the aunts, who'll want to know what I did in London, while you attend to Lavinia and all the

other business. And, I say, Joan! Let's go to bed
early—very early! You're about done in, with all
that's happened to-day, and it's not so long since
you were down with measles. I wonder it hasn't
been too much for you."

"I'm all right, but I am tired," Joan owned.
"A long night in a proper bed wouldn't hurt you
either, Jandy Mac! But I couldn't sleep unless I'd
done something about Vinny Miles."

"Run along and ease her mind," Janice agreed.

CHAPTER XI

A VISIT FROM LAVINIA

"THERE'S one more ordeal before us, Jandy Mac. We'd better get it over." Joan, much refreshed by a long night's rest and a reassuring visit to Jen, who was still asleep, looked across the coffee-pot at her visitor.

"Let me guess!" Janice said. "Seeing young Vinny?"

"I shall have to see her sometime. But there's something before that. Guess again!"

"I know. I was thinking about it in bed. You want to go and see if the tree has gone?"

"I don't want to! That's why it's an ordeal. I'm dreading the first sight of the gate-house without its tree. The sooner we get it over the better."

"That tree was rather like a guardian angel to the gate-house, which will now have to stand on its own feet—or, rather, its own foundations!— unprotected from all the winds that blow," Janice remarked.

"It's quite capable of it. I believe we shall like the result, once we're used to it. But it's sure to be a shock at first. Come and help me to bear it!"

"We shall meet Boniface. We shall always meet Boniface when we go through the Abbey."

"That can't be helped. Perhaps we won't see him," Joan said hopefully.

Her trust was justified, for they met no one as they crossed the garth and unlocked the Abbey door. But at sound of the key Ann Watson came out from her room.

"The old gentleman's away down to the village to fetch his things from the forge, Miss Joan. He told me of your kindness. Right pleased and happy he is, to be sure."

"Can you manage, Ann? He won't need a great deal done for him. I don't want to ask too much of you."

"I'll do it. I couldn't say no, and him so set up about living here. He'll be a bit of company for me. It's lonely sometimes. I'm used to it now, but I'll be glad enough of somebody to speak to. He loves the Abbey. We can talk about it."

"I'm glad you feel that way. It's very kind of you," Joan said warmly.

"It will be like having one of the old ones come back to the place—one of them monk chaps," said Ann. "They did use to have old folks living here, didn't they, Miss Joan?"

"Yes, in the infirmary; but there's nothing of it left but a few big stones covered with grass."

"We'll have a 'firmary again for Mr. Boniface— he says that's his name. If he's ill, I'll take care of him."

"How sweet of Ann!" Janice exclaimed, as they went out to the meadow.

"Ann's a very decent sort, and she seems to have absorbed an extraordinary amount of Abbey feeling and tradition," Joan agreed. "Well, what do you think, Jandy?"

"I think you're right," Janice said, as they stood gazing at the stump which was all that was left of the giant elm. "Once we're used to the change, it's going to be an improvement. We can see the gate-house much better now."

"And it's beautiful," Joan said. "Those great buttresses are so strong and simple—so dignified. Yes, I like it. I'm sorry about the tree; I'd never have sacrificed it, if there had been any other way—not even to give us this new, fine view of the gate-house. But Mr. Edwards from the farm insisted that the tree wasn't safe, and that it must go, so I had no choice. And the result is even better than I'd hoped. The gate-house is really very fine, now that we can see it properly."

"It certainly looks able to stand on its own, without any protection," Janice laughed. "I expect it looked like this when Ambrose lived in it. If the tree was there in his day it must have been very young and small."

Joan's face lit up. "That's true. I'll remind Jenny-Wren that we're seeing the gate-house as Ambrose saw it. It will be a real comfort to her."

"You could train creepers over the stump. It looks rather raw," Janice said. "Or it would make a good seat. You've nothing to sit on out here."

"Nobody wants to sit here and look at a rough meadow!"

"Oh, I don't know! That row of trees between the field and the farm is rather fine. What are they? Holly?"

"I believe they're ilex—evergreen oaks. But we don't go near the farm, because Matthew Edwards hasn't been friendly. We keep away from him."

"You could sit and look at the gate-house."

"Yes, and at the tourists driving in from the road," Joan said, laughing. "Here comes one of them! But she's not a tourist. I rather thought she'd come to-day, but she's earlier even than I expected."

"Is it Lavinia?" Janice asked with interest, as the small child with untidy black hair and a red frock entered the meadow from the road.

"Oh, Miss Joan!" She came flying across the grass. "Is she all right—Miss Jen? Oh, thank you for your letter! I'd've cried all night if you hadn't wrote and told me as how she'd get better! It was kind of you to write!"

"She'll be well again in a few days. She isn't badly hurt, but she might have been. Why did you do such a silly thing, Lavinia?" Joan asked severely. "Both you and Jen might have been killed."

Lavinia went very red. "I'm sorry. Everybody's told me what might've happened. I see my Uncle Bonny, and I didn't know as how he was here, and I called to him and then I ran to find him, and that was all, Miss Joan. I didn't think. I never meant no harm."

"By not thinking, you nearly killed both Jen and yourself. It's time you began to think, Vinny. You're a big girl now. I remember you quite well from our drill days, but you've grown a lot, and you look older. You ought to behave as if you were older too."

"Yes, Miss Joan. I'll be careful. Could I—oh, could I see Miss Jen for one minute?"

"Certainly not! The doctor won't allow visitors. Come back in a few days, and we'll see what he says then. It depends how she goes on."

"Yes, Miss Joan, I'll come. I got a present for Miss Jen." Vinny's tone was full of breathless eagerness. She was clutching a battered old black bag, which evidently held a treasure.

"Oh? That's very nice of you. Shall I take it to her?" Joan asked.

"No, please, Miss Joan! I wants to give it to her meself."

"Oh, I see! All right! Bring it next time you come. It's something that will keep, I suppose?" Joan's mind had gone to fresh eggs, perhaps, or something else from the farm.

"It's a book!" Vinny burst out, her face ablaze with excitement.

Joan looked startled and her eyes met Jandy's doubtfully. What sort of book could Vinny possess that could be of the slightest interest to Jen?

"I shouldn't have thought she had a book of her own!" she said to Janice afterwards.

"Miss Jen will like it," Lavinia insisted, reading their thoughts.

"I'm sure she will," Joan said hastily. "It's very kind of you, Vinny. But Jen won't want to rob you of your book."

"I wants her to have it. I ain't got nothing else, only my book."

"Your one treasure!" Joan said. "It's really very nice of you. I'll tell Jen, shall I? Then she can be looking forward to it."

"Yes, please, Miss Joan. But I wants to give it to her meself."

"Of course you must. Jen will be very pleased, and she'll want to thank you. Bring the book in a few days, and then I hope we'll be able to let you see her."

"Yes, Miss Joan. And Mrs. Jaikes, she said as how I was to give you this." She fumbled in her bag and drew out an envelope.

"Thanks very much, Vinny; and thank you for bringing it. That's a real help." Joan took the letter. "Now don't worry any more about Jen. We're taking care of her. Would you like to see your Uncle Bonny? But I'm afraid he's out; he's gone to the forge to fetch some things. He's going to stay in the Abbey, so you'll see him another day."

Lavinia's eyes wandered to the stump of the old tree. "Did they have to kill it, Miss Joan? It were so big and pretty, and such a nice shade. You used to sit under it and tell us things."

"It had to come down, Vinny. It wasn't safe. We all felt bad about it, but it couldn't be helped."

"Looks ugly now," Lavinia said gloomily.

Joan laughed. "I used to sit under it. Now I'm going to sit *on* it!" And she perched herself on the raw stump. "Does it still look ugly, Vinny?"

"No, Miss Joan. Looks all right now." Vinny's eyes dwelt on her adoringly.

"Then don't be silly! Don't think any more about it. Run along to the village and speak to Uncle Bonny before you go back to the farm. And—I say, Vinny! Go into the shop and buy some toffee to take home with you!" And she slipped sixpence into Vinny's rather grubby hand.

Beaming, Lavinia ran off, hugging her bag, and left Joan and Janice looking at one another.

"I'd give something to see what she has in that bag!" Joan said yearningly.

"How can a dirty little scrap like that have a book that Jenny-Wren could possibly want?"

"That's what I'm wondering. It's probably a tattered copy of *The Three Bears* or *Cinderella*. I'm glad to have the chance to warn Jen. She might have had a shock."

"Lavinia doesn't look bookish! She's a weird little person."

"Jen has a present for her too. We bought it in the village yesterday; red ribbon to tie back that untidy hair. Jenny-Wren's idea is that nobody can feel decent or have any self-respect with her hair all in a mess."

"I'm sure Jen's right. Lavinia might look more like her grand name, if she were tidy."

"She's merely Vinny at present," Joan agreed. "I was carrying the ribbon in my handbag when the accident happened, so I've left it in Jen's room; she must present it herself. I'd have liked to tell Vinny she was untidy, but what use would it have been? I'm quite sure she's never had a pretty hair-ribbon in her life."

"What is in the letter she brought, do you suppose?"

"Oh, that! It's the address of Lavinia's father in America. Jen and I think he ought to send for her; he's been there for years—since she was two, to be exact—ten years. And there are several big brothers. Vinny isn't wanted at the farm. She ought to be with her own people. Surely they could afford to keep her now!"

"It may not be keeping her that will be difficult, but getting her there," Janice remarked, as they walked back through the Abbey. "How could a scrap like that go to America? They'd need to come and fetch her, and that would probably be impossible."

"I know; it isn't easy. But if they really wanted her, they might find a way."

"It doesn't look as if they wanted her very much."

"No," Joan admitted. "She's rather a little stranded waif. And she'll remain one, unless somebody does something about it. Mrs. Jaikes talks of writing to the father, but I don't believe she could do it, and Vinny certainly couldn't do it herself—not without help."

"So you and Jen feel it's up to you to take on the job?"

"We could help her to write to her father. The first step was to make sure of the address."

"Couldn't old Boniface write for you? He's related to them, isn't he?"

"Hardly related—just a sort of connection. Vinny's mother was his niece. He's an uncle by marriage to her father, isn't he? It's not much of a relationship! And, anyway, Jandy Mac, *does* Boniface look like a letter-writer?"

Janice laughed. "I can't say he does. His letter to his son in Birmingham will probably take him a week. I wonder if the son will be able to read it?"

"Jen and I will write a better letter to Mr. Miles than Boniface would do."

"You certainly will! Good luck to you—and to Lavinia! You must tell me the end of the story when it happens. I shall have gone back to Sydney by then."

"You may be Mrs. Fraser before we get Vinny pushed off to New York," Joan agreed. "I suppose we shan't see you for centuries once you're married?"

"I'm very much afraid not." Janice looked down at her ruby engagement ring. "We'll probably live in Samoa. It's very beautiful, and Alec's ship will call there often, when he's going round the Islands. Make the most of me while you have me, Joan-girl, for I'm not likely to be in England again for a long, long time!"

"You'll be bringing up a large family—the little girl who is to be called for me, as a start."

"I won't forget," Janice grinned at her. "The first girl is to be called Joan. Perhaps I'll have Jen and Joy afterwards. But you must find somebody and get married too, and then you can call your first girl Janice."

"I will. But I see no sign of its happening, so far," Joan retorted. "Come and see if Jenny-Wren is awake. We must tell her about her book!"

CHAPTER XII

SIR KEITH RINGS UP

"A BOOK? Vinny Miles wants to give me a book?" Jen stared up at Joan in dismay. "How lovely of her! But how ghastly, Joan! What do you suppose it will be?"

"I suggested it might be *The Three Bears*," Joan laughed. "You'll have to be thrilled and grateful. Whatever it is, it's Lavinia's very greatest treasure."

"I'll be pleased all right! I think it's frightfully touching that the kid should want me to have it. But I'm glad you've warned me. I'll have time to get used to the horrible idea. Perhaps it's a school book—arithmetic or spelling—and she's terribly bucked to have one of her own. Fancy wanting to give it to me! Did you give her the ribbon?"

"Certainly not! It's your idea and your present. In any case, I hadn't it with me. I agree with you: her hair's dreadful, all over the place like that. She'll look a different girl when it's tied back neatly."

"I believe she'll be quite pretty," Janice said. "But she's a scarecrow at present."

"A scarecrow in the Abbey," Jen grinned.

"Tell me about the tree, Joan and Jandy. Has it gone? Does it look too awful?"

"It doesn't look too good, unless Joan is sitting on the stump. Then it doesn't look at all bad," Janice told her.

Jen's eyes went from one to the other. "Tell me what you mean. Don't be pigs, you two!"

"The gate-house looks much better than it did. It's really beautiful now." And Joan sat on the bed and explained Jandy's joke.

"There's another thing, Jenny-Wren. Boniface came to ask for you last night, so I told him he could come to live in the Abbey, if he'd like it. Both he and Ann seem pleased with the idea."

Jen bounded up in bed, and then sank back with a groan. "I forgot! I'm sore all over. Oh, Joan, really? How lovely of you! It will be wonderful to think he's there, being the aged and infirm, looked after by the monks! You and Mrs. Watson are the monks. Oh, I'm so glad! It adds something more to the Abbey—a lovely thing!"

"Perhaps it does, but you aren't supposed to get excited," Joan scolded. "I oughtn't to have told you yet."

"I'm excited all right! It's a thrilling happening for the Abbey! Mrs. Watson doesn't mind? Then it's quite perfect. And every time we go into the Abbey, he'll be there and we can talk to him. What's the matter? Why did you look at Jandy Mac like that?"

"Because, to be honest, that's the part of it I'm

not sure about," Joan confessed. "We go into the Abbey to be quiet and think, not to talk to old men, however nice they are."

"And he'll always be there." Jen grasped the point. "But I don't believe he'll be a nuisance. You can say you don't want to talk. He'll understand."

"Miss Joan is wanted on the telephone." A maid appeared at the door. "A call from the Manor."

"The Manor? How very odd!" Joan rose quickly.

"It must be from my friend, Sir Keith March-wood. Give him my love, Joan!" Jen called after her.

"Isn't Joan a brick, Jandy Mac?" she said, when they were alone. "Giving up her own little place to old Boniface, and letting him be always there, when she'd heaps rather have the Abbey to herself! I know how she feels. But I don't think Boniface will be much of a disturber to her. I'm not here all the time, of course; it matters far more to Joan. I do think she's marvellous!"

"I quite agree, Jenny-Wren. But tell me about the man at the Manor. What did you call him? And why is he your friend?"

"Sir Keith Marchwood. Jacky-boy and I tres-passed in his house and found the pictures of the Abbey church. He was jolly nice about it; he might have sent for the police or flung us out. It's a long story; I'll tell you some day. Or you can ask Joan to tell you and to show you the pictures. Just now I'm wondering too much what he's saying to her."

"For an invalid who isn't to have any excitement, you aren't doing too badly, between Lavinia and Boniface and Sir Keith Marchwood," Janice observed.

Jen grinned. "There are always things going on where I am," she said complacently.

"I wish to speak to little Miss Jen," the baronet was saying. "Is she staying with you, Miss Joan?"

"Yes, she's still here," Joan began doubtfully. "But I'm afraid she can't come to the telephone. She's upstairs in bed."

"Could she come to see me for a few minutes this morning? I have something that may interest her, and I am returning to town shortly."

"I'm sorry, but she can't do that. She has had a slight accident, and she has to keep quiet for a few days."

"Please tell me what has happened! I like that child."

"She ran out just as our big tree by the gatehouse was being felled, and was knocked down and badly bruised. No bones are broken, but she has to stay in bed and rest."

"Tut! I hope it isn't serious?"

"He sounded really annoyed," Joan told Jen later. "I assured him it wasn't serious, but that it might have been. He asked if you were allowed to have visitors, and if he could see you if he called for a few minutes on his way back to town. There seems to be something he is very anxious for you to see, and he wants to show it to you himself. I said you weren't supposed to have any excitement or to see people, but that we would let him see you, if he'd be kind enough to call."

"I should think so!" Jen exclaimed, her eyes wide with amazement. "What on earth can it be? Gosh! Fancy Sir Keith Marchwood getting all excited about seeing me!"

"Perhaps he's found a book for you," Janice laughed. "If he has, I guess it will be more thrilling than Lavinia's book is likely to be."

"He's coming at twelve. Till then, Jenny-Wren, you're going to rest," Joan said. "Jandy and I are going to leave you to be quiet."

"I'd heaps rather talk. I shall only lie and worry about Sir Keith," Jen said rebelliously.

"There's nothing to worry about. I shall come at half-past eleven to do your hair and make you look neat and tidy."

"Make me look very beautiful for the baronet! You might put it that way, Joan."

Joan laughed. "Come along, Jandy Mac. She's talking too much. Would you like a cat to keep you company, invalid?"

"I'd like the Mother Superior. She's fat and sleepy and she purrs so loudly."

"I hope she'll help you to go to sleep." And Joan went to find the stout, placid mother-cat, who lived in the Abbey, but came often to the house for extra tit-bits.

"Don't ask me what Sir Keith is talking about, Jandy Mac!" she said, as they left Jen and the cat in one another's arms, whispering words of comfort and content. "For I haven't the slightest idea. There are all sorts of things in that old house—the Manor, you know—and he seems to be going through his treasures. He has found something that he thinks will interest Jen. That's all I know."

"It's likely to be a bigger thrill than Lavinia's mysterious present," Janice said. "Tell me about Jen and the baronet! Things have been happening while I've been in Scotland—things besides measles!"

"We couldn't write to you because of the measles quarantine. And Jen had Jacky-boy here for company and had no time for letters—except letters to baronets!" And Joan laughed and told the story of Jen and Timothy Spindle, whom she called her Stowaway; and then led Janice to the Abbey, to see, hanging in the refectory, the pictures of the great church.

"Oh, Joan! How wonderful to have these and to know just what it was like!" Janice cried.

"Yes, they are real treasures. Jen and Jack are so proud of having been the ones to find them. And Jen has a real friendship with Sir Keith. How I wonder what it is he wants to show her!"

"Jen is wondering, too," Janice laughed.

CHAPTER XIII

A BOOK FOR BABY KAT

"WHAT is the meaning of this, Miss Jen?" Sir Keith had climbed the stair slowly and rather painfully, and had dropped into a chair by the bedside.

Jen, flushed and eager, with very neat yellow plaits framing her face, looked up at him and laughed. "I'm sorry to be in bed! It's terribly kind of you to come. I somehow managed to get under the tree just when it was toppling over, but there's not much the matter with me. It banged me in a lot of places, and they're still rather sore, but I haven't broken any bones."

"Tut, tut, my dear! How could you do such a silly thing?"

"Well, you see, it was really somebody else who was silly," Jen said confidentially. "A girl from the village, called Lavinia Miles—but we call her Vinny—saw her uncle standing there, and she hadn't known he'd come. She was surprised, and she forgot all about the tree and ran to him. I saw her and I thought for sure and certain she'd be killed, so I sprinted after her and shoved her out of the way, but I didn't get quite clear myself. She was all right, but the wretched tree crashed down on me. I thought my last moment had come! It was rather beastly, though I haven't told Joan. She thought it might have broken my back, and so did the men. It was really awful for all of them. I didn't know any more till I woke up in the house. They'd carried me on a stretcher, or a gate, or something."

He looked down at her curiously. "I see. You were more heroic than clumsy, in fact."

"Why did you want to see me?" Jen demanded, thinking it time to change the subject.

"I have something to show you. I am going through certain old treasures at the Manor. My brother Andrew, who is my heir, does not understand them as I do and might not know their value. It seems better that I should look through them while I am still able to do so." Under Jen's keen gaze, he hurried on to the real subject of his visit. "I have found a book which I think may interest you."

"A book!" Jen murmured, her eyes gleaming with laughter. "How simply priceless! It's all right, Sir Keith. Somebody else is going to bring me a book too, but I'm certain sure yours will be much nicer than hers. What sort of book is it?"

"A book of drawings, done by our ancestress, Katharine Marchwood, about the time——"

"Katharine, who married Peregrine Abinger when she was only fifteen, and came to live here and was Joy's ancestress too?" Jen gave a small shriek of excitement. "Oh, Sir Keith, you don't mean that Katharine drew pictures and that you've found them?"

"She was clever with her pen—the sort of pens they had in those days. She even painted a little." Sir Keith was unwrapping a flat package he carried.

He laid a portfolio of big sheets, loosely bound together, on Jen's knee. "Look, little Miss Jen! On the outside she has written: ' For my Baby Kat, if she be a girl-child.' I imagine she did these drawings before her first child was born, and intended them for her."

"My Baby Kat!" Jen murmured, fascinated. "Didn't she call her Kitty or Kathy?"

"Short names were fashionable at that time. You find Bet for Betty and Peg for Peggy, and Sue and Sal and Poll and Pen. Katharine might very well call her baby Kat."

Jen grinned. "It isn't very polite. Oh, Sir Keith, may I look at her pictures for Baby Kat?"

"Some are not very interesting—just sketches of the garden and the dogs and horses. But Katharine was really gifted, and some of the drawings are true to life. I will show you why I say they were probably done in the first year of her married life."

He turned the big pages, yellow with age, and Jen had glimpses of dogs and horses, trees and flowers.

"Look!" he said quietly. "Katharine was not very good at figures and no good at all at faces, but the suggestion of this drawing is plain enough."

A buttress of a great building, which was obviously part of the gate-house—a small tree— an old man vaguely sketched in, but definitely with a long white beard and wearing a loose robe and a hood—and a flock of tiny birds around his feet. Under the drawing was written, in thin spidery characters: "Brother Ambrose and His Small Ones."

"Oh!" Jen whispered, and lay and stared at the picture and then at Sir Keith. "A picture of Ambrose at last! Oh, Sir Keith, how simply marvellous! You can't see much of him, of course, but still it is Ambrose! Oh, call Joan! We must show Joan!"

"'His Small Ones' suggests that Ambrose was a lover of birds," said Sir Keith. "There is a drawing which seems to show he cared for animals also."

He turned the pages and found another drawing, in which the same old figure, sitting under the same small tree, seemed to be talking to a little creature, who sat gazing up at his raised finger, fluffy tail curled round neat, tiny feet.

"Is it a cat?" Jen whispered. "What has she written under it? It's difficult to read. What does she say?"

"As far as I can make out, she says: 'Brother Ambrose and His Strippit Cat'!" said Sir Keith.

"'Strippit'? Do you think they stripped cats,

as they do dogs in the summer? They couldn't pull their fur off! Though I often think cats would like it, in hot weather," Jen added.

"I think Katharine means ' striped '; a striped cat—a tabby. You can see markings on the animal."

Jen peered at the drawing. "It is! Oh, it is! Ambrose had a little striped cat for a friend! Oh, Sir Keith, isn't that wonderful? He sat under a tree and talked to her! I believe he's scolding her or preaching a sermon; perhaps she'd been after his Small Ones! Oh, how glad I am to know all this! Please call Joan! We must tell her!"

"Ambrose died about two years after Katharine married young Peregrine and came to live here. That is why I say the drawings must have been done in the early days of their married life. Their first child was a daughter—Baby Kat, I presume. A son and heir came later."

"I wonder if Katharine was good to the little striped cat, for Ambrose's sake! And if she fed his birds—his Small Ones! I do like her name for them!"

"I expect it was his name for them. Miss Jen, I must go. I have to return to town. I will ask Miss Joan to come to you, and you will show her the pictures."

"May we keep them for a little while?" Jen asked wistfully. "We'll be just terribly careful of them! I'm dying to show them to Joan, but Joy will be crazy to see them too, and she's away at the seaside. Katharine was her ancestress, not Joan's, you know."

"The book is for you," said Sir Keith. "Do what you like with it, but keep it safely, for it is interesting and precious."

"For me? For us?" Jen gave a shout. "Do you really mean that? Are we to keep it?"

"It was returned to us, with other possessions of Katharine's, after her death. I do not think Andrew or Kenneth would value it. I am sure you will. It is in its right place here, where the drawings were made."

Jen's eyes were blazing. "We'll keep it in the Abbey, with the other treasures. I won't take it away; I shall give it to Joan. That's what you mean, isn't it?"

"That would be best," he assented. "Now get well quickly! I don't like to think of you lying in bed. I prefer to see you turning head over heels in moments of excitement."

Jen blushed. "I'm afraid I did do just that, didn't I? I'm awful sometimes, I know. I'd have liked to do it to-day, because of this lovely book, but it would hurt quite a lot. I shall look at the pictures while I have to stay in bed. Sir Keith!" she called, as he reached the door.

"What now, little Miss Jen?"

"I haven't said thank you," Jen said breathlessly. "But I do thank you, a thousand million times, and Joan and Joy will thank you too."

"I am glad you are pleased. I thought the drawings would appeal to you."

"Pleased! I'm jumping about with happiness—inside me, you know. And the pictures will be the greatest possible comfort to me while I have to lie in bed," she added.

"Good! That will make me very happy. Good-bye for the present, little Miss Jen."

CHAPTER XIV

ST. FRANCIS IN THE ABBEY

"JOAN! Come and look!" Jen said very quietly, almost reverently, as Joan came into the room, after seeing Sir Keith to his car. She spoke so gently that Joan knew something had moved her greatly; Jen the excitable was quietest when her feelings were most deeply touched.

"What is it, Jenny-Wren? Sir Keith said you had something to show me."

"Ambrose!" Jen gave a subdued whoop of joy. "Let me inform you, Miss Shirley, that Brother Ambrose loved birds and fed them and called them his 'Small Ones'. And that he had a little striped—I mean strippit!—cat, and he used to preach to her, sitting under a small tree beside the gate-house. Oh, Joan! Could it be our huge tree that knocked me down, do you think?"

"What are you talking about, Jen, dear?" Joan asked anxiously. "Has Sir Keith's visit been too much for you? You look all flushed and hot. We told you not to get excited!"

Jen gave a trill of happy laughter. "Anybody would be excited! Look, Joan! Ambrose and his little cat!"

Joan sat on the bed and gazed at the drawing.

"Oh, Jen, dear, what is it? Who did it? It certainly looks like Ambrose!"

Jen explained in breathless haste: "Drawings by Katharine, who married Peregrine. For her baby girl, before little Kat was born. Look, she says so! Sir Keith found them, and he's given them to us. He said they were for me, but that would be silly. I'm not going to take precious family documents to Yorkshire! I shall give them to you."

Joan was looking through the book, her eyes filled with wondering reverence. "What a treasure! Drawings from Tudor or Stuart days! Oh, look, Jen! Have you seen this one? Ambrose sitting under the tree and calling the little cat, and she's running to him, with her tail straight up! Ours have run to me like that dozens of times. Katharine could draw cats!"

"She wasn't much good at faces. I love that one!" Jen gloated over the sketch. "Is it our tree, Joan? It would be marvellous to know it had really been Ambrose's tree!"

"It's in the right position, for that's certainly a bit of the gate-house. I'm sure it's our tree," Joan agreed. "What a pity it had to come down!"

"But you sat under it; Vinny said so. You were just like Ambrose, sitting under the tree!"

Joan laughed. "It was a very small tree in his day. We must show Jandy, and we must tell Joy. She'll be thrilled to have a gift from her ancestress.

Jandy Mac! Come and look at Sir Keith's discovery!"

"Sir Keith seems to have thrilled Jen quite a lot," Jandy said severely, coming to sit on the bed also. "We ought to put ice on her head and darken the room, and go away and leave her to be quiet, taking the discovery that has been so exciting and enjoying it downstairs by ourselves. What is it, anyway?"

"Don't you try!" Jen retorted. "It's still mine; I haven't given it to Joan yet. I'm going to gloat over it till you let me get up."

"What an angel kitten!" said Janice. "But what a funny old man! The cat's good, but he's a very poor attempt. Who is the artist?"

Jen and Joan explained together, a breathless jumble of Joy's ancestress, the fifteen-year-old bride of Peregrine, who had been Ambrose's adopted son in his last days—of Baby Kat, before she was born—of Ambrose and his birds and little striped cat—of the big tree that had just come down.

"Gosh, that's interesting!" Janice exclaimed. "It really is a treasure! Let me look at it properly!"

"I haven't been through it yet." Jen, feeling suddenly tired, surrendered the drawings. "See what you can find, Jandy Mac. Joan found a lovely picture of the 'strippit' cat."

Janice turned over the pages, eager for a discovery on her own account. "I'm glad to have seen this for myself. I'd never have understood, if I'd only heard of it in letters. The lady couldn't draw faces; she always pulls Ambrose's hood over his head—clever of her! But she's good at creatures—dogs and horses and birds. Here's Ambrose talking to a squirrel." And she held the page for the others to see. "It's sitting up, holding something in its hands and nibbling; lovely bushy tail! It isn't interested in the sermon, but it's not a scrap afraid of the old chap."

"That's a happy thought," Joan said. "We've always felt he was a dear, gentle old soul. It's nice to know the wild things loved him."

"What's that funny word written under the squirrel?" Jen peered at the ancient writing.

"' L'Ecureuil '. It's plain enough."

"But what does it mean? Was it the squirrel's name?"

"It certainly was," Joan laughed. "' Ecureuil ' is the French for squirrel. Ambrose was half French, you know."

"I never heard squirrel in French before. I wonder if Ambrose called him ' l'ecureuil '?"

"Very likely. And I expect his name for the birds, the Small Ones, was really Les Petits."

"I like that!" Jen exclaimed. She turned a page and gave a squeal of delight. "Oh, Joan, look! Here's the cat sitting on a bit of broken wall, with her feet tucked under her so that you can't see she has any—what Joy calls ' her hands in her muff '. She has beautiful dark rings round her neck, like chains of beads—absolutely regular. Look, Jandy Mac! Her eyes are half-shut, and Ambrose, still with no face but with a long beard again, is tickling her behind her ears; she's loving it. I do like that one!"

"Perhaps the cat was ' he '. Why should a monk have a lady friend?" Janice teased.

"I'm quite sure she's a little girl. Look at the tiny dainty legs and feet in that other picture!"

"She has a lovely tail, almost like the squirrel's. Find something else, Jandy Mac," Joan said, keeping a careful eye on Jen, however.

Janice took the book and began to look through it. "I say! These are different—these end pages. I don't believe the lady did them. Look, Joan! Very careful drawings of bits of architecture; lovely close work, quite different from Mistress Katharine's cats and creatures. Isn't this the rose window?"

"In the sacristy?" Joan exclaimed. "Of course it is! Who did these? They're not Katharine's style at all."

"There's a squiggle in the corner of each of them!" Jen gave a crow of delight. "I believe it's a signature, a sort of monogram—two or three letters all mixed up."

"You're right," Janice said. "Each of these drawings of places has your squiggle in the corner; and, what's more, they're all details of small bits of buildings. Could they be studies for the paintings of the church, Joan?"

Joan was examining the drawings carefully. "They're bits of the Abbey," she announced. "This is the odd little piece of stone carving under the refectory; I'd know it anywhere. This is the lavatory arch, on the outside of the refectory."

"Of course it is!" Jen shouted. "Who did them, Joan? Who put those squiggles in the corners? It wasn't Katharine; she drew cats and squirrels. And none of her things have squiggles."

"Katharine's pictures were done for her children," Joan reminded her. "They wouldn't care about bits of an old building, but they'd love her birds and creatures. Someone else drew these studies in her book."

"She lent it!" Jen gave a characteristic cry of delight. "She lent it to that man who came to do the paintings of the church! These are his sketches, before he started on the big pictures! And he did little bits of the Abbey, when it was in ruins, in case Henry came back and bashed the rest all to pieces! Oh, Joan, don't you think it's true?"

"I do," Joan said, her face lighting up. "I believe some of these are the famous artist's studies and sketches, jotted down in the end part of Katharine's drawing-book. It was she who brought him here to paint the church, from Ambrose's descriptions. I expect they were friends, and she lent him her book."

"I don't suppose books for drawing were too

plentiful in those days," Janice added. "It sounds very likely. But we can prove it, you know."

"Prove it? How?" Joan and Jen looked at her quickly.

"If he took the trouble to sign his sketches, with what Jen so beautifully calls 'squiggles', wouldn't he sign the paintings too?"

"Of course he would! Come and look!" Joan started up.

"I can't come," Jen wailed. "Go and find out quickly, Joan and Jandy!"

"You sprint off to the Abbey and find out, Jandy Mac." Joan controlled her excitement and sat down on the bed again. "See if there are monograms on the pictures of the great church! You know where I keep the Abbey keys. No, I'm not coming; it doesn't need two of us to look for squiggles! I'll see them next time I'm in the refectory. Do, please, go quickly, Jandy! We're aching to know!"

With a swift look at her, Janice raced away.

"You stayed because of me," Jen cried. "Oh, Joan, why did you? I'm not a baby! I could wait!"

"So can I wait," Joan assured her. "I'm not in a hurry to see the signatures, but I do want to know if they are there. Jandy will tell us. I never noticed whether the paintings were signed or not; it's such a very small squiggle that it's quite easy to miss it. But now that you've discovered it, Jandy will see it if it's there. Once she has eased our minds, we're going to leave you to rest. You're very tired. If the doctor comes he'll scold me. You will rest and be quiet, won't you, Jenny-Wren?"

"I'll try," Jen promised. "I am tired, but it's been so thrilling, Joan!"

"Too thrilling for to-day, but I don't see how we could have refused to let Sir Keith come. We won't look at the book any more just now; it's much too exciting! It will keep. We'll enjoy it later on."

"May I hold it, if I definitely don't open it or look at it at all?" Jen pleaded.

"If you promise faithfully that you won't look inside, I'll leave it with you," Joan agreed. "You don't want to feel Jandy and I are discovering things in it that you haven't seen, do you?"

"I didn't mean that. I just want to feel it's there and to think about it. But if you'd like to take it——" Jen began.

"That's generous, but we won't do it. It's yours, and you must make the discoveries, if there are any more. I expect we've seen most of it now. Well, Jandy Mac?"

"A perfectly clear signature in the corner of each painting, but as impossible to read as Jen's squiggles," Janice reported. "They're monograms, but I've no idea what the letters were."

"That doesn't matter. The great thing is that we know we have the artist's sketches for his pictures, in Katharine's drawing-book."

"I don't think Sir Keith knew. He only spoke about Katharine's bit," Jen said.

"Then you must write and tell him. He may not have examined the book carefully right through. Now, Jandy, we're going to leave Jenny-Wren to rest and dream about Ambrose and his little striped cat."

"'Strippit cat'!" Jen said reproachfully.

"And high time too. She's had far too much excitement for an invalid," Janice scolded.

"I say, Joan!" Jen called, as Joan reached the door. "Don't you think Ambrose was rather like St. Francis? It's marvellous to have a St. Francis of our own in the Abbey! I don't know if he really preached to the birds—I mean, Les Petits!—and the little cat and the squirrel, but I'm sure they liked him. Perhaps I'll call one of my boys Francis."

"That's better than Boniface, anyway," Joan remarked.

"What's all this?" Janice asked. "Is Jen planning her family already?"

"She's going to have ten boys," Joan said solemnly. "She threatened to call one Boniface, but I said it would be unkind."

"Brutal!" Janice agreed.

"Not ten boys! I said ten children. Three of them had better be girls. I like boys best, but I must have some girls too."

"Dear me!" Janice said. "You're going to be busy!"

"That's what I said," Joan laughed. "Yes, perhaps Ambrose was like St. Francis—that's another thing for you to think about! But go to sleep, Jenny-Wren, and don't look at that book any more just now."

"All right, I've promised. But I shall go right through it this afternoon. I'm sure there are things in it we haven't discovered yet," Jen said drowsily.

CHAPTER XV

VINNY'S MYSTERIOUS BOOK

JEN SPENT a happy and, it must be admitted, an exciting afternoon turning the pages of her book. Katharine Abinger's chief concern had been to draw subjects that would interest her children while they were small, and many of the sketches were of animals and birds. But one or two were treasures, and Joan, coming in at tea-time, found Jen chuckling with delight.

"Look, Joan! See what I've found! Ambrose, with his face all hidden by his hood, as usual, walking along pulling a string behind him, and the little cat running after it! Wasn't it nice of him to play with her? There's something written under it, but I can't make it out."

"It was just like Ambrose to play with her, I'm sure." Joan came to look. "I've quite a new picture of the dear old chap. Isn't she pretty, with her dark stripes and her fine tail? But what's this? ' Ambrose and Minet.' That's what it looks like to me."

"I thought that too. What does it mean?"

"Minet is the cat's name," Joan announced, after a moment's thought. "We should spell it ' Minette '; I expect it's a French name for a cat.

There, Jen! We know the name of the little strippit cat! She was Minette."

"Oh, marvellous!" Jen cried. "I'm glad you've guessed! And Minette had a baby. Look!" And she turned another page, to show Minette with a tiny dark object at her side. "Do you think Ambrose was pleased?"

"They should be called Min and Minette," Joan laughed. "That's a real addition to Ambrose's family!"

"To our Abbey family," Jen added. "I'm glad to know Minette had children. There's an odd picture here, Joan. Look! It's called 'The New Rosary'. Ambrose, still with no face, is holding a chain of beads. What would a lay-brother do with beads? And what's a rosary? If this was a new one, he must have had an old one!"

"What a string of questions! Don't you know what a rosary is? Oh, Jenny-Wren!"

"Ought I to know? But why should I?"

"You're keen on the old monks. A rosary was a bead chain they used to help them in their prayers. Everybody had one—not only the monks."

"Oh!" Jen thought this over. "Oh, well! If it helped them, I suppose it was all right. Did Peregrine give Ambrose a new one?"

"It looks like it. I wonder what happened to his old one? It's not the sort of thing anybody would lose."

"Perhaps it was worn out."

Joan shook her head. "I'd have liked to have Ambrose's rosary. It wouldn't wear out. I don't know what could happen to it."

"Perhaps he left it lying about and somebody stole it."

"Nobody would—unless, maybe, the squirrel!" And Joan laughed. "Suppose Ambrose was praying, with the rosary, under the little tree, and someone called him away in a hurry—to see somebody in the village who was very ill, perhaps. He put down the beads, and the squirrel thought they were nuts—they may have been brown wood—and took them and buried them in some corner. You know how squirrels love to bury things!"

Jen grinned. "He'd get a shock when he dug them up and tried to eat them in the winter! And Ambrose was terribly upset because he couldn't find his beads, so Peregrine and Katharine gave him a new rosary."

"We can't know, but it seems quite a possible story," Joan said. "The squirrel would be the most likely thief. Nobody else would rob old Ambrose! See if you can find any more stories!"

The book was a great comfort to Jen during the next day or two, while her bruised limbs made movement difficult and painful. She lay turning the pages and gloating over the drawings, and she wrote letters of warm thanks to Sir Keith and of excited description to Joy.

"It's keeping me from the awful thought of

Vinny Miles presenting me with a book," she said frankly to Joan and Janice. "I can't worry over Vinny while I'm thinking about Ambrose and Minette."

"Is it such a dreadful idea?" Janice asked.

"Frightful! I'm sure the book will be something utterly ghastly, and I won't know what to say."

"It may not be so bad," Joan said hopefully. "It may be an old Bible or prayer-book of her mother's. If it's old enough, it may be quite interesting."

"A hymn-book!" Jen wailed. "I know it will be a hymn-book, with ' Dare to be a Daniel ' and ' Pull for the Shore ' in it!"

"Those don't sound like hymns," Janice protested.

Joan laughed. "Moody and Sankey, Jandy Mac. Jen's probably right. It's just the sort of thing Lavinia and her family would treasure."

"I've seen them in cottages in the village at home," Jen said. "There's ' Let the Lower Lights Be Burning '—about light-houses, I think. I rather like that one. And ' Hold the Fort, for I am coming '—that's a good one too. But I don't want Vinny to give me hymns! It's worrying me quite a lot."

"We'll soon put an end to that," Joan told her. "Vinny comes to ask for you every day. You'll really have to see her soon. She's sure you must be better now."

"I'm not better enough for hymn-books," Jen asserted. "Have you given her the ribbon yet?"

"No, I was leaving that for you to do."

"Then give it to her, Joan, dear, and tell her how to wear it. I don't want to see her any more with her hair all in a mess. Tell her it's from me, if you like; but make her look decent before I see her again!"

"I will, if it's what you want, of course. I'll show her how to do her hair," Joan promised.

That evening she went to Jen's room and sat on the bed. "Something to tell you, Jenny-Wren."

"Something nice? Where's Jandy Mac?"

"Writing to Alec. I had a talk with Boniface to-day. He's had a letter from his son."

"And will they let him stay in the Abbey?"

"They think it's a splendid plan. It's quite plain, from the letter and from what he says, that they are badly overcrowded, and they'll be really glad for him to live somewhere else, so long as he's sure he will be happy."

"He'll be happy all right." Jen had been thinking of Boniface while she lay in bed. "He wants to stay."

"Yes, but it's a long way from his people."

"He'll like it. The question is, will you be happy, or will he spoil the Abbey for you?"

"He hasn't been any bother so far. I asked Ann to give him a hint that I came into the Abbey to be quiet, and he has never come near or disturbed me in any way. I had to send Ann to find him when I wanted to speak about his son; she told me he had had the letter. But I haven't been in the Abbey very much since he came."

"For fear he'd want to talk." Jen understood at once. "I'm sorry about that, Joan. And you've lost your little room."

"We can't have everything. Boniface and Ann seem to be quite good friends, and he's radiantly happy, so it's worth while giving up my room to make that possible. But there's something on his mind—something he won't tell me."

"How odd!" Jen exclaimed. "Has he committed a crime?"

"Not that sort of thing. There's some idea in his head, but he won't speak of it. Perhaps he'll tell us some day. When I asked if he'd like to stay in the Abbey, he implied that there was somewhere else he'd like to be, but that it wasn't possible, and that was all he would say. He didn't mean Birmingham, with his son; there's somewhere else."

"Gosh, how weird! Where do you suppose he wants to go?"

"I haven't the slightest idea. I could write and ask his son if he knows, but it doesn't seem fair. Boniface would tell us, if he wanted us to know."

"I thought the Abbey was what he wanted most of all."

"There's one thing he wants more than the Abbey, but he's either ashamed of wanting it or shy of speaking of it. He just says it isn't possible."

"You might make it possible. Then he'd go away, and you'd have your room again."

"I thought of that. But I shan't ask him. If he tells me, that will be different. There's something we ought to be doing, Jen—nothing to do with Boniface. We ought to make up a letter to Vinny's father, now that we have his address."

"Won't Vinny write herself?"

"She must, of course, but I think we should write too. I don't feel Vinny's letter will be quite enough."

"I think it will be a lot too much!" Jen hinted. "If her letter is anything like I expect it to be, he'll come galloping home by the first boat to take her back and teach her how to spell."

"That would be one way out of the difficulty. We'll send a letter from her—you may be sure of that! But it would help to have one from us too. I've been making notes. Would something like this do?

"'DEAR MR. MILES,

"We have seen your little girl, Lavinia, or Vinny, and she does not seem to be happy at the farm. You will know that her aunt has died and she is left alone. Mrs. Jaikes has been very good and has done what she could, but she has a family of her own and her hands are full. Would it not be possible for Vinny to join you and her brothers? She is old enough to be some help to her stepmother, and she would like to be with her own people. If no one can come to fetch her—and we realise that might be difficult—perhaps we could find somebody who would take care of her on the journey, if you could send the money for her fare. We would make arrangements and would see her safely on to the ship, if you could meet her at Montreal.'"

"Montreal! I thought it was New York!" Jen exclaimed.

"The address is 'Whiteways Farm, Ontario, Canada.' Vinny said America, but she was wrong, or else they've moved."

"It's all the same to her," Jen grinned. "It's the other side of the Atlantic, and that's America. Somehow I'd rather she went to Canada than to New York, and a farm would be jolly for her, as she's used to farms. They've called their place after the village here! That was nice of them. Vinny will go from one Whiteways to another! It's a jolly good letter, Joan-Queen. I can't think of a single other thing to say. He must send her fare, of course. You can't pay it!"

"It wouldn't do to suggest it," Joan said decidedly. "If they don't want Lavinia they'll make an excuse, and she'll have to stay where she is. If they want her, they'll manage to send her fare. If we paid for her and sent her to them, they might not welcome her."

"Of course, they must say they want her," Jen agreed. "I do hope they'll be kind! Tell her to write her letter at once, Joan. Then we can send them together, and then we shall know."

"I'll tell her to write it in pencil and let us see it," Joan suggested. "If it's too bad, we can improve it and then she can copy it out neatly."

"It won't be Vinny, if you edit it! Send it just as she writes it, *I* say! Then he'll know the worst!"

"We'll see how bad it is," Joan decided. "I haven't asked him to pay something to Mrs. Jaikes. I'm hoping he'll think of it for himself."

"Much nicer," Jen agreed.

"If he doesn't suggest it, we shall have to ask him. It would be only fair," Joan said.

She came to Jen's room later in the day to report progress. "Vinny nearly wept with joy when I gave her the ribbon. She begged me to thank you 'everso'. I told her to divide her hair into two and tie each bunch with ribbon, and I helped her to do it, for the first time. It improves her enormously; she looks a different girl. She says she can do it herself, and she's thrilled by her own appearance. She's coming to-morrow to show you how she looks. I said you'd be able to see her, unless you had a bad night, for any reason."

"Meaning, unless I worry too much about that awful book and can't go to sleep!" Jen laughed. "Kind of you to leave me a way of escape! But I won't take it. We'd better get it over and know the worst. I promise faithfully I won't shriek with horror. I'll be pleased, whatever it is."

"It's Vinny's dearest treasure. I know that by the tone in which she speaks of it. So I hope you will be pleased."

"I oughtn't to take it, if she cares as much as that," Jen began hopefully.

"Oh, you must take it! She's determined you shall have it."

"What did she say about the letter to her father?"

"She thinks mine is just everso lovely. She was terrified at the thought of writing one herself, but I talked to her, and she's promised to try. She'll do her best and bring it to show us to-morrow."

"Horrors in store for us!" Jen groaned. "Oh, well! We'll get them all over at once!"

"The mysterious book is old; she let fall that hint. Very, very old, she said. I do wonder what it is!"

"I expect she just meant that it was in rags and tatters, all dog-eared and dirty. I know it's an ancient hymn-book!" Jen sighed. "Don't look at me when she gives it to me, Joan, dear! I shall shriek with horror, or roar with laughing, or sob, or something, if I catch your eye."

"It isn't likely to be as old or as interesting as Katharine's book, I'm afraid," Joan said sadly.

CHAPTER XVI

LETTERS, AND A DIARY

THE next morning brought letters for everybody.

Joan handed a fat one to Janice with a smile. "From your Alec. I'll take Jen's up to her; it's from her mother. Mine is from Joy. I want to know what she says about her ancestress Katharine's present to us."

"Joan! Come and speak to me, Joan!" Jen hung over the gallery railing, a few moments later.

Joan dropped Joy's letter and ran upstairs. "Anything wrong, Jen, dear?"

"I don't know." Jen looked at her with anxious eyes. "Mother starts by telling me about the wedding, and then she breaks off to say Father is ill and he won't be able to come home just yet, and do I think you could possibly keep me for a few days longer? Or I can go back to The Grange, but I'll be all alone there. I don't want to do that; I'd worry about Father if I had no one to talk to. Oh, Joan, dear, may I stay here with you?"

Joan flung an arm round her. "Jenny-Wren, of course you'll stay here! Don't think twice about it. Write to your mother at once and say we'll love to keep you for as long as she likes."

"She doesn't feel it's fair to ask you, after last summer," Jen whispered, clinging to her. "There's a note enclosed for you. I expect it's to apologise. You had to keep me for a fortnight last August. Do you remember? But she doesn't know what else to do, and she feels so happy about me while I'm here, she says."

"What a lovely compliment! I'll write to her. I think she knows we love having you."

"*I* think she's worried about Father." Jen hid her face on Joan's shoulder. "I know I am. He oughtn't to be ill again. Do you think there's anything badly wrong with him, Joan?"

"I expect the travelling and the excitement of the wedding have upset him a little," Joan said consolingly. "A few days' rest may put him right. Are they staying with friends?"

"Yes, but if he isn't better soon, she'll think he ought to go to hospital. They can't be a nuisance to people," Jen said brokenly. "I'm frightened about him, Joan. Suppose he doesn't get better?"

"Oh, Jen, dear, there's no need to think of that! Wait for a day or two. I expect good news will come soon. Get dressed now, and then you can write to your mother. Remember you have to be ready for Lavinia, and she's sure to come early."

"I don't like Father to be ill so often."

"But he was better quickly after that last time, and he's been all right through the winter, hasn't he?"

"Yes, but he shouldn't be ill again, Joan "

"I don't expect it's anything much. Shall I help you to dress?"

"No, I can do it; I'm almost all right again. You read Mother's letter. I'll be down soon."

"There's a letter from Joy," Joan said, in an effort to cheer her.

It was successful, to some extent. Jen asked eagerly, "What does she say about Katharine's pictures?"

"She's thrilled to the limit, and Mother wants to see them too. Joy's so pleased about Minette and Ambrose! You shall read what she says when you come downstairs."

"We must cheer Jen up," Joan said to Janice, as she told her the news. "She's really worried about her father."

"What's wrong, do you think?"

"I've no idea. He seems to have these bad times, but the last one was a year ago, and it passed off safely. I hope he'll be all right. Jen's too young to have any serious trouble. I'd be sorry if she had to grow up too soon."

"We'll keep her from thinking," Janice promised.

Jen was quiet and shadowed at first, but she became more herself in her interest in Joy's comments on her new treasure, and when Lavinia appeared she was able to greet her with a shout of delight.

"Vinny! Oh, you do look nice! You've done

your hair quite beautifully! I didn't think you were so clever!"

"Red suits Lavinia," Janice remarked.

"Oh, Miss Jen!" Vinny ran to her. "Be you all right? They all tells me as how you might've been killed, and it had oughter been me."

"I'm sure nobody ever said anything so horrid!"

"I expect they told Lavinia it might have been her," Joan said. "Jen's much better now, Vinny. Doesn't she look all right?"

"Yes, Miss Joan. Oh, Miss Jen, I were frit when Uncle Bonny said you looked just like a dead lass!"

"Oh, Vinny, dear! Don't think about it any more! I never was anywhere near being dead!" Jen cried. "Turn round, so that I can inspect you properly! Is your back as neat as your front?"

"She was very near being dead." Joan's eyes shot a meaning look at Janice.

"But if she doesn't realise it, don't rub it in," Janice murmured.

"Very nicely done!" Jen said, with warm approval. "Does Mrs. Jaikes like you like this?"

"Said I weren't quite such a scarecrow," said Lavinia bluntly. "I done my letter, Miss Joan."

"It was clever of you to be so quick. May we see it?"

Shyly, Lavinia produced a sheet of paper and watched anxiously as the girls looked at it together.

Joan's face lit up in relief. It might have been so very much worse. Lavinia, apparently, could spell, though her English grammar deserted her when she spoke at full speed, as she often did. The writing of the letter had been an ordeal, and she had done it slowly, taking great care, and had made it very short.

"DEAR DAD,

"Let me come! I want to be with you. I will be a good girl and do everything you say. I will work hard to help my new mother. I can do lots of things in the house, and I know about babies. Please let me come to you, Dad!

With love from your girl,

LAVINIA (VINNY)."

"What a lovely letter!" Jen cried. "Vinny, you really are very clever!"

"She's done it splendidly," Janice said.

"If I were your father, Vinny, that letter would make me want you very much," Joan exclaimed. "It's exactly right."

Lavinia looked from one to the other doubtfully. Then her face lit up in immense relief. "Be it good, Miss Joan? I didn't know what to put."

"It couldn't have been better, if we'd told you what to say," Joan assured her. "You know, Vinny, you ought to try to talk better. You can do it. That letter is quite well put together, and you use the right words. But when you talk you often use the wrong ones."

"I f'get, Miss Joan, when I talks quick."

"Quickly." Jen flung the word at her. "An adverb, not an adjective."

Lavinia stared at her blankly. "Sounds like school."

Jen laughed. "Vinny, are there any cousins in Canada? Didn't we hear that your dad and the boys went out to join an uncle, who was doing very well?"

"That be right, Miss Jen. Uncle Jim, he's got a farm, and my dad went to help him, as his boys wasn't old enough to be of use."

"Boys! Then there are cousins." And Jen eyed Vinny thoughtfully. "I'm glad they're boys."

Joan looked at her quickly. Then she turned to Lavinia. "Vinny, has your new mother any children? You said something about taking care of babies."

"Mrs. Jaikes says as how the last letter what come—came!"—poor Vinny pulled herself up under the horrified eyes fixed on her—"said there was a little girl. She'll be my sister, won't she? I'd love to have a little sister; I haven't never had one."

"I hope Mrs. Jaikes is right and there is a baby half-sister," Joan said gently. "You'd be a great help to them; you'd take care of her beautifully. Now, Vinny, what about that book you were going to give to Jen?"

"I ain't brought it, Miss Joan. I were frit. It beant good enough for Miss Jen."

"*What?*" There was a united shout from the three.

"Oh, Vinny, you brute!" Jen wailed. "I want my book!"

"Vinny, how unkind!" Joan cried. "Didn't you know we'd want to see it?"

"She might have let Jen say if it was good enough," Janice said indignantly.

Lavinia looked from one to the other, startled by their outcry. "It's old," she faltered. "'Tain't anything much. It were wrote by Jane Miles long ago—her whose dad had to run away or he'd've been hanged, so they do say."

Stunned, Jen stared at Joan, and Joan stared at Lavinia.

"Hanged?" Janice murmured, dazed. "What for? Was he a sheep-stealer?"

"Not sheep," Lavinia protested, shame in her voice. "But he were a bad 'un, and he had to run."

"Or he'd have been hanged. It must have been serious," Janice began.

"If they'd catched him, but they never did," Vinny added.

"Jane Miles was his daughter?" Joan started to straighten out the story. "And she wrote a book, Vinny? What sort of book?"

"'Bout the things she did, Miss Joan."

"Do you mean a diary?" Jen gave a shout. "Oh, Vinny, do you mean a diary? Joan, it may be thrilling! For it must go back a long way. Everybody has forgotten this gentleman who ought to have been hanged. It must be centuries ago!"

"*Do* you mean a diary, Vinny?" Joan demanded.

"I d'n know. What's that, Miss Joan?"

"Make her fetch the book. Then we'll see for ourselves," Janice suggested. "I hope it's safe!"

"It would be ghastly to lose it now and never know what it had been!" Jen was breathless with eagerness. "The book's safe at home, isn't it, Vinny?"

Lavinia stared at her, puzzled by all the excitement. "I did think as how it were too old to be any good and I'd just burn it," she began.

"Vinny! But you didn't do it?" Joan cried.

"Oh, Vinny! Say you didn't burn it!" Jen was almost in tears. "You couldn't do such an awful thing!"

"Ease our minds, Lavinia!" Janice implored. "Is the book still safe?"

"Yes, miss. I didn't do it. I thought I'd ask you first. I knows as how Miss Joan likes old things."

"Oh, thanks be!" Jen gasped. "I'd have died if we'd never seen that book!"

Without a word Joan went to the telephone.

They all gazed after her, Jen and Janice tense with suspense, Lavinia alarmed and bewildered.

Joan returned in a moment. "Vinny, Mr. Clarke, from the village, is coming round in his

little car. He uses it as a taxi, you know; our car
is at the seaside. He's going to take you to King's
Bottom to fetch the book. We'll tell you whether
you should burn it or not. You'll bring it to us,
won't you?"

"You said you were going to give it to me!"
Jen urged.

"I'll do it, Miss Joan. I'll give it to Miss Jen."
Lavinia was obviously a little frightened and very
much puzzled. "But it ain't nothing to fuss
about. It's just the things she did every day."

"Even if it's only, ' Helped Mother in the dairy
—Fed the hens—Picked peas—Played with the
cat,' it will be interesting, because it happened so
long ago," Jen explained, her eyes eager.

"Wouldn't you like to go with her in the car,
Jandy Mac? Then you'd see her farm," Joan
suggested.

"I'd love it! I'll see she doesn't burn that
book!" Janice ran upstairs for her coat.

"Don't you want to go, Joan?" Jen asked
wistfully. "I'm afraid I can't. That wee car on
farm roads would bump too much, and it would
hurt. You'd see the book sooner if you went."

"You and I are going to wait here till Lavinia
and Jandy bring the book," Joan assured her.

"We won't look at it or talk about it till we've
brought it back to you," Janice promised. "Here's
the car. Come on, Lavinia!"

CHAPTER XVII

JANE'S SECRET HOUSE

JOAN looked at Jen anxiously. "This is far too thrilling for a semi-invalid! Calm down, Jenny-Wren! It will be fun to read Jane's old diary, but it isn't likely to be important."

"It's better than the hymn-book!" Jen chuckled. "We guessed a lot of things, but we never thought of a diary! It's a real thrill! I'm so glad her name was Jane. It's the same as you, and me, and Ambrose's Jehane ; lots of Janes!"

"Jane Miles isn't connected with the Abbey. Jen, who do you suppose her father was?"

Jen stared at her. "*I* don't know! Do you? How can you know? A farmer who did something so awful that he ought to have been hanged, but who ran away and escaped, leaving Jane behind. That's all I know about him!"

"They hanged people for theft in those days. It doesn't mean he was a murderer. Don't you think he may have been our highwayman, who hid his booty in the Abbey?"

Jen leapt up with a shout. "Of *course* he was! Oh, Joan, how clever of you! The thief who robbed Katharine Marchwood of her locket and purse up on the hills! And we found them in the

Abbey, and you gave them to me! I'm sure that's who he was!"

"I think so," Joan assented. "We didn't know what had become of him, but evidently he fled from the country. Perhaps he heard people were coming to take him, and he had no time to go to the Abbey and search for his wallet, with the rings and pearls and things."

"I expect he had some others tucked away," Jen grinned. "I say, Joan, you don't think the jewels ought to belong to Lavinia, do you? She's his descendant, I suppose. But I don't want to give her my little blue ring!"

"They were stolen goods," Joan reminded her. "Lavinia has no claim on them. But I think it would be a reason for helping her to go to her father, if he makes any difficulty about her fare."

"Oh, she must go to Canada! Because of those cousins, you know."

"I was going to ask what your look meant when she said she had cousins, and why you were so glad they were boys."

"You know quite well! They're sure to want to marry her, and then she'll be nicely settled, with a house of her own. She's jolly pretty, now that her hair's done properly."

"It would be a happy way out for Lavinia," Joan admitted. "But we can't arrange it."

"We can hope for it, and we can make sure she goes to live with them, and we can tell her to write to us," Jen retorted. "I hope it happens.

Oh, I wish they'd hurry! I'm aching to see my book!"

It was not long before the car came racing up the beech avenue, but it seemed a long time to Joan, and a very long time to impatient Jen.

Janice jumped out and pulled Vinny after her. "There, Lavinia, take that book to Jen quickly! It's safe, Jenny-Wren!"

Jen sat on her couch, her eyes blazing with excitement, her hands outstretched. Joan, standing by, watched her anxiously.

Lavinia ran to her and thrust a parcel into her hands.

"My aunty found it in the attic, and she give it to me and said as how it wasn't nothing to do with Mr. Jaikes, but it belonged to the Miles people, and my name was Miles; hers was Browning. I'm giving it to you, Miss Jen, because you been so sweet to me," she said, all in one breath.

"I didn't know I'd been sweet, but it's marvellous of you to think so, Vinny Miles!" Jen tore away the paper and found a small leather-bound book.

With a little gasp, she opened it and showed a great many blank pages and a few covered with tiny, crabbed writing.

"She didn't go on doing it." Lavinia watched her anxiously. "She wrote it at the beginning, and then she stopped."

Janice grinned. "A lot of us are like that with

diaries! I've started ever so many, but I never went very far in any of them."

"Look!" Jen whispered. "Inside the front cover: ' *Jane Miles. Her Book. King's Bottom Farm.*' Doesn't it make her seem real?"

"Are there any dates?" Joan asked.

"Only the month—February or March or April. She doesn't trouble to put the year," Jen said sadly. "It's too bad of her, and very lazy."

"Very slack. We ought to know what year it was," Janice said severely.

"It's a disappointment, but we can't have everything. Read us bits, Jen! Is it about feeding the hens and playing with the cat?"

"That sort of thing. The first bit she's written is: ' *My puss has three black kits in the barn. I shall take one to my house.*' Why would she take only one to the house?"

"I expect the mother cat lived in the barn," Joan said.

"The house would be much nicer for them! Then she says: ' *Played at my house all day. Nobody knows. It is my own place.*' What does she mean, Joan?"

"I've no idea. Surely everybody knew her house?"

"Here it is again: ' *Went to my house. No one can find me there. Took pan, and a plate, and a knife. Mother says they are lost.*' Joan, what is she talking about?"

"It sounds as if she was furnishing a secret

place," Joan said. "I'm afraid Jane had something of her father in her, if she took household goods and let her mother think they were lost."

"A secret!" Jen chuckled. "A hiding-place, where no one could find her, and where she played house. This is sport, Vinny! Your ancestress was a bad girl, but she was rather fun. Listen to this bit: '*Took potatoes to my house, and an old jug, cracked, but it holds water, and a cake.*' She was going to have a picnic! I wonder if she made a fire and cooked the potatoes?"

"She couldn't eat them raw," Janice remarked. "I wonder where the secret place was? Jane seems to have been very human! It's just what any small girl would love to do."

"She takes '*a curting*'. Would that be a curtain?" Jen asked. "Oh, yes! The next thing is '*a cushing*'—cushion, I suppose! They must have missed—oh, she owns up! Oh, good! Listen, everybody: '*Told Mother about my house. She gave me a rug and a pail and a spoon.*' So her mother was nice about it!"

"I expect Jane had taken so many things that she had to confess. What an understanding mother!" Joan said. "I wonder if the black kitten went there too?"

Jen turned the page. "It isn't easy to read; the writing's so tiny. Here she says: '*In my house all day. Mother bothered about Dad. Told me to go and play and not come back till dark.*' Oh, do you think they were getting worried about him?"

"The highwayman, Jandy Mac," Joan said quickly. "Don't you think it's very likely?"

"I hadn't thought of that. Sure to be!" Janice exclaimed. "They were afraid the police were on his track and that he'd have to go, and they wanted Jane out of the way. Any more, Jenny-Wren?"

Lavinia stared blankly. The reference to the highwayman was beyond her, but she realised that the girls were pleased and interested about her book.

"A little more. Jane writes next day: ' *Mother cried again about Dad. He didn't come home last night. She don't like his goings-on.*' I bet she didn't, poor soul! Here's something else: ' *Mother says Dad will have to go away, to France or somewhere. She cries and cries. She tells me to go to my house every day.*' They wanted to get rid of Jane."

"I wonder where this mysterious house was?" Janice pondered. "Some distance from the farm, evidently."

"Jane had no idea what her dad had been doing. Here's something odd: ' *Took Peter to my house. Must go each day to feed him. Left the others with their mother.*' Joan, who was Peter? Did she steal him too?"

"Don't you think he was the black kit?"

"He was! He was!" Jen shouted. "The very next day she says: ' *Went to feed Peter. He caught a mouse. Not hungry. Caught mice all night, maybe.*' The secret place must have been overrun with mice. She's cooking at last, Joan: ' *Made fire and boiled potatoes. Water from fish-stream. Dad told me——*' The fish-stream! She couldn't mean—Joan! What does Jane mean?"

"What did her dad tell her?" Joan demanded, looking startled.

Jen read on hastily: "' *Dad told me the Old Ones kept their fish in the stream, but I never saw any.*' The Old Ones! Joan!" Jen gave a cry. "The Old Ones would be the monks! It was our fish-stream! Joan, the secret house must have been in the Abbey! Oh, Joan, is it true?"

"It sounds very much like it!" Joan exclaimed. "After all, we know the Abbey was a heap of ruins at that time. What better place could there be for a child's secret play-house? I expect Jane found some corner that wasn't too messed up, and cleared it out and made her private place there. What a wonderful bit to add to our Abbey history!"

"The highwayman's daughter playing house in some corner, while her dad fled across the sea," Janice added. "A new story for you, Abbey-girl!"

"I wonder where it was? Yes, it's a real addition to our pictures of the Abbey," Joan said happily.

"It's just marvellous!" Jen's quiet tone was reverent. "We had story-pictures of the Abbey when Jehane and Ambrose were young and in love; and we thought we had a picture of it when Ambrose was old and lived in the gate-house, and the Abbey was in ruins. Then Katharine's book made that picture real and gave us Minette and her baby, and the squirrel and the birds, so that we have stories for that time too. But we've had nothing about the Abbey for all those centuries when it was cluttered up with rubbish and farm stuff—except the highwayman hiding his stolen goods in the tunnels underground. Now we know that Jane Miles had found the Abbey, and had made a secret place in some corner and played house there with Black Peter! Isn't it wonderful, Joan?"

"It's very satisfying," Joan said. "Vinny Miles, your book is a treasure. May we really keep it? It belongs to the Abbey, you know."

"It's for Miss Jen, please."

"That means it's for the Abbey." Jen beamed on her joyfully. "It will be kept carefully as a very precious thing, Vinny. We'll write in it: ' *Given to the Abbey by Lavinia Miles.*' Then, when you're across the sea, people will remember you and little Jane."

"Oh, Miss Jen! I'd like that terrible much!"

"Is there any more?" Joan asked. "Can't you find out whereabouts the secret house was?"

Jen turned to the book again. "There's a little more, but I don't know if it will help. Here's another bit: ' *To-day made my house bigger by moving the apples. But I hope Farmer Edwards will not come.*' Because he'd see she'd been messing about with his apples, I suppose!"

"Apples!" There was meaning in Joan's tone. Jen and Janice looked at her.

"What's up, Joan-Queen?" Jen cried.

"Do the apples tell you anything?" Janice demanded.

"The story is that the day-room was used for keeping straw in, and the chapter-house for storing apples," Joan explained, her voice exultant. "Jane's secret place was in a corner of the chapter-house."

"How clever of you, Joan!" Janice exclaimed.

"How lovely to know!" Jen cried. "I shall always think of Jane when I go into the chapter-house now! I can just see her, pushing the apples away and putting down her rug and her cushion and hanging up the curtain—to make a sort of tent, perhaps—and making a little fire and cooking, and crawling under the curtain and feeling safe from everybody. She must have been very fond of her house!"

"She probably spoiled the apples, by pushing them all into a heap," Janice laughed. "Apples aren't supposed to touch one another."

Jen sat fingering the little book, while Lavinia gazed at her in deep content. Vinny did not understand the story in the least—it would have to be explained to her carefully by Jen and Joan—but she knew that her gift had satisfied the girls, and it made her very happy.

"There's a little more of the diary." Jen came

out of her dream, to find Joan and Janice watching her also. "We'd better read to the end. I wonder why Jane stopped?"

"Most people get tired of writing diaries," Janice remarked.

"I say, there's a story here!" Jen gave a chuckle of delight. "Listen, all of you: ' *To-day Dad came to my house. Mother told him to hide in it, because they were after him. He hid with me and Peter all day. I went to fetch water and I saw them looking for him, but they did not come, and he was safe.*' Just a heap of ruins! Why should they come?"

"And the highwayman was lying snugly in a corner of the chapter-house!" Janice laughed. "Well, well!"

"The Abbey was harbouring a fugitive, who had sought sanctuary there," Joan began, her eyes lighting up. "We can't approve of the highwayman, but I'm glad he wasn't found hiding in the Abbey."

"Joan, what a lovely idea!" Jen cried. "An ancient stowaway in the Abbey! I am so thankful they didn't find him!"

"You're sure they didn't?" Janice asked, while Joan sat dreaming over this addition to her Abbey's history.

"No, he got away that night. Jane helped him; she says so. She adds: ' *Dear knows if we shall ever see him again.*' I don't suppose they did, poor things!"

"No, he wouldn't dare to come back. Perhaps

Jane went to France and joined him," Joan suggested.

"Her didn't," Lavinia said suddenly. "Her's in churchyard here. ' *Jane Miles, aged fourteen,*' it says."

"She died soon after she wrote about her secret place," Jen whispered. "She was only my age. Well, I'm glad she had her house to play with. I'm sure she loved it. And it helped to save her father's life. That's the end of her story. Perhaps she didn't go back to it after he'd gone away."

"Perhaps she stayed at home to comfort her mother," Joan said.

"There's something else in that book," said Lavinia suddenly.

"I've read it all!" Jen cried. "What do you mean, Vinny?"

"I'll show you, Miss Jen. I d'n know what it means, but I thought as how maybe you'd understand."

Lavinia took the book, and the three girls crowded closely round her to see what she would do.

CHAPTER XVIII

JANE'S SECRET MAP

"LOOK!" said Lavinia. "A sort o' pocket place at the end."

The back cover of the book had been slit carefully, to leave a gap between the lining and the outside. Vinny's fingers slipped in and drew out a folded paper.

"It was hers—Jane's. Her name's on it," she said.

"Yes, there it is!" Jen almost whispered in her excitement. "'*Dad gave this to me and told me to keep it safe, for it would bring me luck. But what it means I do not know.—Jane Miles.*' Gosh! Didn't the highwayman explain?"

"He hoped to come back," Joan said. "Or he had to go in a hurry. He'd meant to stay another night, and he'd have told her more, but she came back from fetching water and told him she had seen 'them', and he decided to go that night. What is the paper, Jen?"

"We're good at making sense of mysterious documents," Janice urged.

Jen unfolded the paper and spread it on her lap. The three girls stared at it and then looked at one another blankly.

"There isn't much of it," Joan began.

"I can't make anything out of that!" Janice wailed. "The only thing I can say is that it bears a remarkable family likeness to the maps I brought home."

"That's hopeful. For we made out what they meant and found treasures," Joan exclaimed.

"But there's far less of this one! It's only two lines and a spot."

Jen gazed at the marks on the paper and frowned. There were two long lines, one straight, one wavy. Between them was a small cross. On the straight line there was a square, level with the cross and shaded with slanting lines.

"It's paths," Jen announced at last. "Or roads. And an important spot between them, marked with a cross. Perhaps the highwayman buried something special, that he had found or stolen. The two roads meet here at the bottom of the map; it *is* a map, of course. There's a line drawn across, where they meet. They make a sort of long V, with the important spot between them." She looked at the elder girls doubtfully.

"That sounds all right," Janice agreed. "Go on, detective! You were the one to read my maps, by guessing the steps properly. Do you remember? You set us off on the right track. What about these scribbles?"

"I can't read them," Jen said hopelessly. "Where can we find two roads coming together like a V? That's not the way roads usually behave! And what's the spot between them? You

don't expect to find a cross marked on the grass,
I suppose?"

Try as they would, the girls could find no clue
to the map. "We need Joy," Joan said. "It might
suggest something to her. She knows every inch
of the countryside."

"We can't wait till she comes home!" Jen cried.
"Jandy Mac may have gone back to her Alec, and
I may be in Yorkshire. I jolly well hope I shall
have gone," she added, her face clouding at the
memory of her mother's news.

"Could we send it to Joy and ask what she
thinks?" Janice began.

"We might send a copy, and in the meantime
we could go on thinking about it," Joan suggested.

"I'll copy it. There isn't much of it," Jen said.
"I'll do one exactly like this, and we'll keep the—
what do you call it, Joan?"

"The original." Joan supplied the word.
"Right, Jenny-Wren! You make a careful copy,
and I'll write a letter telling Joy how we found
it. I can't tell her all about Jane and her book,
but I'll say a little. Lavinia, you run along home
and copy out your letter to your father. It's
exactly right, but we can't send that pencil
scribble, you know. Copy it in ink. I'll find you
some good notepaper."

"I'll put at the end, ' Miss Joan give me the
paper,' or he won't understand."

"Yes, that's sensible. But say ' gave me ',
Vinny; be careful. Bring the letter to-morrow

morning; it can go inside mine. I've written to him too. Now, everybody, get to work! I must start on my letter to Joy, for it will need to be a long one."

"And what is little Jandy to do?" Janice demanded.

"Write to Alec!" There was a united shout from Joan and Jen.

Janice grinned. "I could answer this morning's letter. I love talking to Alec. See you later, then!"

With a board on her knee, Jen worked carefully at her drawing. Joan, writing at the table, glanced at her occasionally, relieved to see her so much more like herself, and, in spite of the news about her father, so enthralled by this new interest.

Jen looked up suddenly. "Joan-Queen!"

"Yes, Jenny-Wren? Have you discovered something?"

"I don't believe both these long lines are roads. They're different."

Joan came to bend over her. "What do you think they are? You've done the copy very carefully."

"This one isn't straight. It wanders about just a little. Perhaps it's a river."

"That's an interesting idea." Joan sat beside her and looked at Vinny's map closely. "I see what you mean: it's a wavy line, and the other is straight. A road and a river meeting at a point:

it's quite a different place to look for! Your idea may be important. But where have we a river that meets a road?"

"We haven't even many rivers. We've plenty of roads. I think my idea makes things worse," Jen said dejectedly.

"It gives Joy something more to think about," Joan pointed out. "Any hints we can give will help her. Has anything else occurred to you?"

"That shaded square place might be a house or a barn. It's on the road-line, not the river one."

"That's a good thing! The road's more likely to have a house beside it than the river—if it is a river."

"If!" Jen groaned. "It's a puzzle, all right. The road seems to go right through the house—if it is a house! It's all across the road."

Joan laughed. "Don't sound so despairing! You've found out quite a lot, just by concentrating on the map while you copied it. I'll give you another point! If your wavy line is really a river—if it is!—then that thing at the bottom, where the road and river meet, may be a bridge."

"A stroke through the river-line, where the road crosses it!" Jen cried. "Oh, how clever! I'm sure it's a bridge!"

"You write down all these ideas for Joy, while I tell her about the book. I haven't nearly finished yet." And Joan brought a writing-pad. "Anything we can suggest will be useful to her. I wish we knew what that cross stands for!"

"It's where he buried something."

"I think so too—something that would bring Jane luck. But what are we to look for? Suppose we find the road and the river and the bridge, and perhaps a house, we'd like to go on and find the buried treasure. But what are we to look for? We couldn't dig up yards of field or road!"

"There might be a bush, or a pile of stones, or a post," Jen pleaded.

"I'm afraid they'd have vanished. It must be a hundred years since Jane wrote her book. If we find all the rest of the map, we'll see if there's anything to guide us. But don't get too keen, Jen! If we do find this place, we couldn't just go and dig! It would be somebody's land, you know."

"But they'd let us search for buried treasure, wouldn't they?" Jen asked in dismay.

"It would depend whose land it was. Matthew Edwards, at Bell's Farm, certainly wouldn't have us digging in his fields."

"I know he's an old pig. And why it should be called Bell's Farm I can't imagine!"

"We've all wondered about that. But no one can tell us."

"But wouldn't the highwayman bury his secret in one of his own fields?"

"I don't know, Jenny-Wren. And I'm not at all sure that Mr. Jaikes would want us digging up his fields or his farmyard. He has nothing to do with Old Miles, the highwayman."

"If we find the place, I shall go and ask whoever it belongs to, to let us have a try."

"Then I hope, for your sake, it won't be Mr. Edwards. You'd better write and tell Joy all these thoughts. I must finish my letter." And Joan went back to her work.

CHAPTER XIX

UNCLE BONNY'S SECRET

LAVINIA came early next morning, a neatly copied letter in her hand.

"Good for you, Vinny! That's very nicely done," Joan said. "We'll post it at once, with my letter to your father, and a letter to Joy about your map."

Lavinia, glowing with pride and importance, stood rubbing one foot on the other leg in an embarrassed way. "Mrs. Jaikes says as how she hopes my dad will have me. And Uncle Bonny says so too. I come through the Abbey, Miss Joan, and I tells him about the letters. You said as how I could go that way."

"I did," Joan agreed. "So Mr. Browning thinks you should go to Canada, does he?"

Lavinia's foot rubbed up and down harder than ever.

"She'll spoil her stockings," Jen said suddenly. "If you must do that, you should have bare legs, Vinny."

"Mrs. Jaikes won't let me, Miss Jen. She says 'tain't proper for a big girl. My Uncle Bonny"— and the cause of Vinny's shyness was revealed in a sudden rush of words—"he says as how he'd like to go too."

"What?" Joan and Jen cried together.

"What's that?" Jandy's head appeared at her window, just above them; they had received Lavinia on the terrace. "Old Boniface wants to go to Canada?"

Jen's eyes met Joan's, their message plain to read. "You'd get rid of him out of the Abbey," they said.

"Lavinia, what do you mean?" Joan demanded. "Your Uncle Bonny couldn't want to go to Canada?"

"But he do, Miss Joan. His girl's married out there, and there's little 'uns what he's never seen. He'd like to go to her more'n anything in the world. But he knows as how it's too far for him, at his time of life."

"Vinny," Joan said sternly, thrusting aside the entrancing suggestion in Jen's excited face, "why do you put ' as how ' into every sentence?"

Lavinia stared at her blankly. "I d'n know no other way to say it, Miss Joan."

"Well, listen! You said, ' He knows as how it's too far for him.' If you said, ' He knows it's too far,' that would be quite enough and it would be good English. What's the use of your ' as how '? "

Lavinia reddened. "I allus says it that way."

"Then it's time you stopped. You only complicate—I mean, mess up!—your sentences. Leave out ' as how ' every time you want to say it. You'll find things are quite clear without it. It doesn't help at all."

"I'll try, Miss Joan. I suppose as how Uncle Bonny—I mean"—hastily—"I suppose Uncle Bonny couldn' go to Canady with me? It's sorter lonely to go all that way alone."

"You wouldn't exactly go alone," Joan comforted her. "If your father can't come to fetch you—or perhaps one of your brothers—we would take you to the ship, and there would be somebody called a stewardess who would take care of you. Your father would meet you. You wouldn't have anything to worry about."

"It'd be nice to have Uncle Bonny there."

"Vinny could take care of Uncle Bonny," said Janice from above, sitting on her window-sill to listen.

Lavinia glanced up, her face alight. "We'd take care o' one another. I wish Uncle Bonny could go!"

"She resisted 'as how' nobly that time," Jen said. "I'm sure it was tempting. Vinny, you look very nice this morning! If you go to Canada, I shall give you yards of ribbon, and you must always do your hair properly. Never leave it in a mess again!"

Lavinia's face glowed. "Nobody never told me I looked nice till you did, Miss Jen."

"Nobody *ever* told me," Jen corrected her. "I think girls should be told when they look nice."

"Some of them don't need it," Janice remarked. "But it won't hurt Lavinia."

"Jandy, do come down! Stop being a voice from above," Joan commanded.

"Could my Uncle Bonny go with me, Miss Joan?" Vinny pleaded. "He wants to see his girl and her little 'uns."

"I'll have a talk with Uncle Bonny. We thought he wanted to stay in the Abbey."

"There was one thing he wanted more than the Abbey," Jen reminded her. "He was mysterious about it. Don't you remember? This is it, Joan."

"We'll talk to Boniface," Joan promised. "You go home now, Vinny, and help Mrs. Jaikes with her babies. We'll see that your letter goes safely; we'll post it at once. Then you must have patience while we're waiting for the answer."

"It'll be a dreadful long time, I'm feared," Lavinia said wistfully.

"Three or four weeks, perhaps. The letter has to find your family after it has crossed the sea, and then your father has to write back to us. But we shall hear some day," Joan said cheerfully.

"Now, Jenny-Wren!" She turned to Jen when Lavinia had gone. "How far can you walk? It's time you had some exercise. Wouldn't you like to post the Canadian letter yourself?"

"Yes, rather! I can go as far as the village, I'm sure."

"If she faints by the way, we'll ask for Mr. Clarke's bumpy little car to bring her home," Janice suggested.

"I'd rather walk," the invalid asserted. "That little rat-trap would shake me all to bits. But you and Joan could carry me."

"Don't you think it!" Janice retorted. "You're a hefty young woman. You'll walk home, my dear!"

"We'll go through the Abbey," Joan said, as they set out. "It's time Jen saw the devastated meadow and the remains of our tree."

"I'd forgotten." Jen looked sober. "Is it very awful?"

"It isn't beautiful. But the gate-house is lovely now. You must think of that."

"I shall think of Ambrose sitting under the tree with Minette and the birds, when it was still very small."

They saw nothing of Boniface as they went through the Abbey. "Out visiting friends in the village," Joan said. "We may meet him somewhere."

Jen stood and looked at the meadow, with the blank space where the big tree should have hung over the gate-house, her face grave. She sighed at last. "I suppose it couldn't be helped. The stump looks awful! Couldn't it be cut right down to the ground? Then the long grass would hide it."

"We'll think about that. Don't you like this side of the gate-house, with those lovely buttresses?"

"Yes," Jen admitted. "It looks awfully fine, but I'd rather have had our tree."

"You've found stories about the tree," Janice suggested.

Jen sighed again. "We must keep the tree and its stories inside us, that's all—in our minds, you know. It's rather like what Ambrose said when he heard Jehane was dead—'I have her in my heart, and she is mine forever'—isn't it?"

"A happy thought, Jenny-Wren! Thanks to the stories in your book, the tree will be ours, in our hearts, for ever," Joan said heartily. "Oh, here comes Boniface! Then we'll ask him about going to Canada."

The old man came in by the gate. Joan, sitting on the tree-stump, called to him as she drew Jen down beside her.

Jen hesitated. "Ought we to sit on it?"

"Of course, silly! Sit here by me and rest, before we go on."

Jen sat silently beside her, looking sober.

"There's room for three, Jandy Mac. Three girls on one seat!" Joan said cheerfully, determined to have no sentimental grieving for the lost tree. "Mr. Browning, Lavinia says you want to go to Canada, to see your daughter and her children. Would you really have the pluck to face the journey?"

The old man stood playing with the hat he held in his hands. "'Deed, Miss Joan, I knows it's too much to think of it, at my time o' life. But my girl, she's over there, and I haven't seen her these ten years and more. Two big lasses and a lad she had when she went away, and now the lasses be married and have little 'uns what I've never seen."

"Great-grandchildren!" Joan exclaimed. "You must be proud!"

"Vinny didn't tell us your grandchildren were married," Jen cried. "Oh, Boniface, you ought to see them before——" She stopped in dismay.

"Before 'tis too late, little missy. Aye, but it be a long ways to go. I'd feared to face it."

"It would be quite easy," Joan assured him, and repeated the plan she had proposed to Lavinia. "We'd take you to the ship and put you on board, and you'd have nothing to do but just wait till you reached Montreal, and your daughter would meet you there and look after you. What about the fare? Would your son help you to find the money?"

"He'd help. I don't know as he'd do it all. But my girl's man has done well. Maybe he'd send something," Boniface began, a great hope dawning in his eyes. "Oh, Miss Joan, if I could see my Annie again!"

"I don't see the slightest reason why you shouldn't see her and live with her," Joan said, her tone briskly encouraging. "I've no idea what it would cost, but I know how to find out. I'll write to people in London, and I'll tell you what they say. You'd only want single fare; you and Lavinia would stay with your families, once you found them. Ask your son if he'd be willing to help, Boniface."

"You wouldn't go alone," Janice added. "Young Vinny would be company for you. Perhaps one person could meet you both and help you to find your way to your families. But they'd have to arrange that on their side of the Atlantic."

"You'd look after Lavinia, wouldn't you, Boniface?" Jen asked eagerly. "It would be wonderful for you both."

"I aren't fit to take care of a little lass," Boniface began. "And it do mean a terrible lot of writing letters and making plans. I'd like to go above all things, but I do think it be too much for me."

"But that's where we would help," Joan assured him. "We could write the business letters, if you wrote to your daughter and your son. You'd have to leave the Abbey, Boniface. I thought you wanted to stay here?"

The old man's face clouded. "I do love the Abbey. But there's my lass and her girls and the new babbies out there, Miss Joan."

"And they matter most. I'm sure you're right," Joan said heartily. "If you stayed here, you'd always be wishing you could go to them."

"Yes, Miss Joan. Could I really go, thinks you? It's a terrible long way."

"But it's a very easy journey—just sitting on a ship! Of course you could go."

"I was feared everybody would laugh and say old 'uns like me should stop to home. But you hasn't laughed. I'll away and writ them letters. Maybe I'll believe it when I hears from Annie that she's wanting me to come." And Boniface stumped through the Abbey, an incredulous look of hope in his eyes.

"He doesn't believe it yet," Jen observed. "He thinks it's a dream. I was afraid he'd back out when he said it was a terrible long way. Then you'd have had him in the Abbey for ever, and it would be my fault, because I said he ought to stay here."

"If he goes, you won't have your aged and infirm person in the Abbey," Janice pointed out.

"But the Abbey will have helped the aged to find something better still," Jen retorted.

"He'll go," Joan said. "His daughter will want him, and we'll encourage him, and I'm sure he'll face up to it. It will be a great relief to Lavinia."

"Of course, I really meant that Vinny would take care of Boniface," Jen explained, as they set out for the village. "But I didn't think it would be tactful to put it that way. I'm quite sure she will. She'll buck him up no end."

"They'll help one another. It's a splendid plan. We'll help them both all we can," Joan promised.

CHAPTER XX

DISAPPOINTMENT

Two DAYS later, Joan was called to the telephone.

Jen and Janice, listening from the hall, heard her give a sharp cry of surprise. "Joy! Joy, where are you?" And then they heard no more.

"In Bournemouth, Joan. Isn't it fun?" Joy spoke at express speed. "I never did a long-distance call before, but it's quite easy. You can hear me, can't you? Then listen hard! I've only a minute or two. We've had your letters, and we're thrilled. You must find out what that cross on the map means! I wanted to come racing home to help in the search, but I decided this would do instead. Joan, try King's Bottom Farm. Go up on the hills—on Long Bottom Hill—and look down on the fields. I believe you'll find what you want. You'll see your map lying below you, if I'm not mistaken. A stream and a footpath meeting, and a footbridge; and there used to be an old haystack on the path—it may be your shaded thing that looks like a building. The field's called the Long Meadow. Good luck to you! I hope you'll find a post or a stone or something to mark the spot. You can't dig over the whole field! I hope the find will be worth having. Ring up and tell me what happens.

Here's our number. Better put it down. Now I'll have to ring off. Is Jenny-Wren all right again? Aunty? Oh, she's splendid! We went to Christchurch Priory to-day, and she loved it. Yes, I'm very fit. Tell me if you have any luck. Good-bye!"

Looking slightly dazed, Joan rejoined the others. "That was Joy, speaking from Bournemouth. I couldn't believe it at first. I've never had a long-distance call before."

"It was just like Joy," Janice remarked. "How are they?"

"Splendid, both of them."

"Joan, did Joy ring up about your letter? Does she know where to find the place on our map?" Jen asked, breathless with eagerness.

"She thinks so. I'll try to remember what she said, but I was so taken aback that I may have missed something. We're to go up on Long Bottom Hill and look down on Vinny's farm, and Joy thinks we'll see our map spread out below us. There's a field called the Long Meadow. It has a footpath, which has an old haystack beside it, and a stream which meets the path, and a small bridge. We couldn't ask for more than that!"

"Not if the stream and the path meet in a long V. What luck!" Jen cried. "Joy is clever!"

"She knows every path and every stream anywhere near us. She's thrilled about this. We're to ring up and tell her what happens. But I think I'll write instead. I can't quite believe I'd find Joy in Bournemouth!"

"I'll ring up for you. I've done it before," Janice promised. "When can we go on this search-party?"

"Can you walk as far as Long Bottom Hill, Jen? It's where we went after we'd been to Vinny's farm."

"Of course I can! I'm quite all right now," Jen said indignantly.

"Then let's go this afternoon. We'll take the map and compare it with what Joy thinks we shall see."

They lay together on the turf of Long Bottom Hill, and Jen held the map firmly because the wind was so strong. Three pairs of eyes, brown and blue and dark, swept over the fields, which lay stretched below like a carpet.

"There!" Three shouts came together.

"I see it!" Janice cried. "Well done, Joy! And there is something between them—a small tree. Is that the spot, do you think?"

"It is! It is!" Jen shouted. "A long V, made by the path and the stream! And the bridge—and the haystack's still there! Oh, come on, Joan! Let's go down! That tree must be where we're meant to dig! It's just where the cross is on the map!"

Joan flung an arm over her to restrain her. "Wait, Jen! It looks like the place all right, and it's just where one would expect Old Miles to bury something, on his own land. But if that tree marks the hiding-place, he didn't know anything about it, so he couldn't have put it on his map.

That's a small tree, and if I'm not mistaken it's a willow, and they grow quickly. That tree hasn't been there for very long."

"Perhaps it was planted instead of an older one that died," Janice suggested.

"It must have been! Perhaps the first tree fell down. Come and dig, Joan! Will they lend us spades at the farm?"

"Jen, dear, do think!" Joan pleaded. "We have to ask leave to dig. We can't rush at Mr. Jaikes's field and begin hacking it to pieces! And I don't really believe——"

"Then let's go and ask him! I'll go, if you like. I said I'd ask! But he'd be much more likely to listen to you."

"What don't you believe, Joan?" Janice asked. "For I don't believe it either."

"That Mr. Jaikes will let us dig, however hard we ask."

Janice nodded. "That's how I feel. He won't believe us."

"But we'll show him the map," Jen urged. "He'll have to believe it then."

"Jenny-Wren, this is going to be a blow, but I must say it," Joan began. "Suppose Mr. Jaikes lets us dig—very unlikely, considering what we know of him, but suppose he does—and suppose we find anything worth while, to whom will it belong?"

Jen stared, her eyes wide with dismay. "You don't mean that old Jaikes would bag it for himself? Oh, Joan, *no*! We'd have found it. Wouldn't it be ours?"

"Mr. Jaikes wouldn't think so. He'd claim anything dug up on his land."

"And buried by his ancestor," Janice added. "Well, not his ancestor! He bought the farm from the Miles people, didn't he? But buried by his predecessor on the land. We wouldn't stand a chance. Joan's right, Jen."

"But it's not fair!" Jen raged. "He doesn't know anything about the treasure! If we don't tell him, he can't possibly find it! At least he ought to go shares with us!"

"A generous farmer might give us a share," Joan agreed. "But not Mr. Jaikes; he's the very opposite of generous. Grabbing all he can get and then trying to get more—that's his character in the village."

"Grasping," Janice remarked. "There's not a hope, I'm afraid."

"Then we won't tell him," Jen said bitterly. "If we can't have it, he mustn't. Joan, couldn't we go at dead of night and dig round that little tree? It's ghastly to see the very spot and not be able to do anything about it!"

Joan shook her head. "I'm not going to dig in an unfriendly farmer's land at dead of night!"

"But don't you want to know what Old Miles buried?"

"Yes, very badly. I'm going to talk to Mr.

Jaikes. If he decides to try to prove our story, he may tell us what he finds."

"If anything," Janice put in.

"If anything. He won't give us a share, but he may let us see the booty, if there is any. It would be better than nothing. You'd like to know, wouldn't you?"

Jen sighed heavily. "Oh, yes! I want to know. But it's so unfair! It's our treasure. Why should he keep it?"

"I don't believe it's anything valuable." Joan tried to console her. "Old Miles told little Jane it would bring her luck. He didn't say it would make her rich. It may have been some old charm or talisman. I don't think it was money."

"Mr. Jaikes may not want anything of that sort. He might let you buy it," Janice suggested.

"When will you go?" Jen asked gloomily. "We may as well know the worst. It's jolly hard lines, when we've found the place and nobody but us knows anything about it! Joy will be wild, I bet!"

"If you'll go home with Jandy, I'll go down to the farm and interview Mr. Jaikes and come home by the village. Lend me the map; I may need it to convince him. See that she has her tea, Jandy Mac! She's not too fit yet."

"Can't we come with you? We might be able to help," Jen begged.

"I'd rather talk to him alone. Honestly, Jen, it will be better. I'll come and tell you as quickly as I can."

Very crestfallen, Jen handed her the map and turned back the way they had come.

A look passed between Joan and Janice. Janice nodded a silent promise to take care of the invalid, and Joan took the track that led down to King's Bottom Farm in its hollow.

She arrived back at the Hall an hour and a half later, and shouted for tea. "I'm nearly dead with thirst! Not a hope, Jenny-Wren. Better forget all about it."

"He won't even tell us, the brute?" Jen asked hopelessly.

"He doesn't believe there's anything hidden. I showed him the map, and he studied it for a long while. I think he wanted to keep it, but I wouldn't allow that——"

"I should think not! The map's ours, anyway!"

"I hope you brought it back safely?" Janice exclaimed. "For Joy will want to see the original."

"I told him that. I didn't say there was a copy. I said Joy might be able to think of some other place that would do as well, and that I must have the map for her."

"It's not at all likely there are two places, just the same," Janice said. "But I'm glad you didn't give him the map."

"He didn't dare to try to keep it, but he stared at it for a long time, as if he were learning it by heart."

"He was!" Jen said wrathfully. "He'll go and

dig at dead of night and not tell us anything about it!"

"I'm afraid he will, but we can't stop him. I'm sorry, but unless you or Joy can think of some other place that fulfils the conditions on the map, we can't do any more. We'll ask Joy; there are other streams and footpaths. But I haven't much hope."

"I haven't any hope," Jen said gloomily. "We've found the place, and that Jaikes pig will dig up our treasure, and we shall never know."

"Here's your tea, Joan," Janice said. "Did you see anything of Lavinia?"

"Not a thing. Mr. Jaikes was in the field, and I went to him there. I didn't go to the house. I hope Vinny was being good and helping Mrs. Jaikes."

"Vinny will be mad, but she won't feel as bad as we do," Jen said heavily.

"Joy will be upset too. Shall I ring her for you, Joan?"

"No, Jandy Mac, I'll write. Thanks very much, but if we speak to Joy she'll want to argue; she'll be sure she could have thought of something else to do. She'll have the letter quite soon. She wouldn't expect us to rush off the moment she rang up, to explore the fields!"

"I think she would. It's what she'd have done herself," Jen groaned. "Joy never waits for anything. She'll ring up again to ask if we've found the treasure."

There was no ring from Joy, however, and the next letter told of a concert to which she and Mrs. Shirley were going that evening. Joy was full of excitement over the map and begged for details at the earliest possible moment.

"She won't like them when she gets them!" Jen said darkly.

She was very silent, and Joan and Janice looked at her anxiously more than once. Jen saw it and said defiantly, "You needn't keep watching me. I'm not going to burst into tears! I feel just sick about things, but I'm not going to howl over them. And I promise you faithfully I won't go and dig up old Jaikes's fields in the middle of the night, unless Joan comes too."

"Joan won't," Joan assured her. "Go to bed and forget our troubles, Jenny-Wren."

"I can't forget, but I'll go to bed." And Jen went sadly upstairs.

"She'll feel better in the morning. She's worn out, poor infant," Janice said.

"I hope she'll sleep. It has been a heavy blow. I'll go and see if she's all right presently," Joan promised.

CHAPTER XXI

A FEAST OF REJOICING

JOAN sat up in bed, startled by a sudden sound. She looked at her watch. Two o'clock in the morning.

"Someone's moving about. I heard a door open. And—there!" at a bumping noise. "I must see what's going on. Perhaps Jen is walking in her sleep—though I've never known her do it. But she was terribly over-excited last night. She may be ill again." She was hurriedly groping for slippers and dressing-gown.

Torch in hand, she crept from her room and leaned over the gallery railing. "Who is there?"

Her light caught a small figure squatting on a rug. "Oh, Joan!" Jen hissed. "Why did you wake? I was being so quiet, and then that pig of a Curate ran at me and got between my legs. If I'd been on the stairs I'd have fallen headlong. Why do you let him roam about loose at night?"

"Because he likes it. What are you doing there? Is anything the matter?" Joan switched on the light and ran down the steps and stood over her. "Let me look at you! Are you ill?"

Jen faced her with excited, laughing eyes. "Did you think I was delirious? I'm all right, but I was hungry, and I thought a biscuit would help. Joy wouldn't like to think of a visitor lying sleepless and starving in her house, Joan!"

Joan stifled a laugh at the reproachful tone. "Jen, what do you mean? Haven't you been to sleep? It's two o'clock!"

"I think I have. How do you know when you've been to sleep? It seems only a few minutes since I was lying thinking about Vinny and Boniface, and Jane and our map, and that pig Mr. Jaikes, and then suddenly I was wide awake. Oh, Joan, I've had the most marvellous idea! I think I must have dreamt it. I was coming to tell you; I couldn't possibly wait hours till the morning! Then I thought if I woke you, you might be hungry, and I knew I was. So I was going to bring biscuits for you too."

"Very kind of you! But I'm going back to bed, and so are you. Fetch your biscuits, but don't bother about me. I'm going to see you and the biscuits safely into your room, and this time you'll please stay there. Then I'm going to sleep again, and I hope you'll do the same."

Jen peered up at her. "Are you cross? I've never seen you cross yet; I didn't think you could be. Are you wild with me, Joan?"

"I shall be, if you aren't back in bed, plus biscuits, in two minutes."

"Oh, no, you won't!" Jen said confidently. "I'm coming into your room to tell you my idea. If you won't listen, I shall go to Jandy Mac. I must tell somebody. I'm far too thrilled to keep it in for five hours."

Joan looked down at her and saw the excitement in her shining eyes and burning face. "Jen, this is absurd! What have you done to yourself? You're all flushed and hot. Are you going to be ill again?"

Jen gave a trill of healthy laughter. "No, Joan, dear, I'm not. I'm quite all right. But there's something I've got to tell you. I can't possibly settle down till I've heard what you say about it. Joan, do you remember thinking I was off my head, when I only wanted to tell you I'd found Ambrose's grave?"

"I remember. You gave me a real fright that night."

"Well, this is just the same. It really is important; perhaps not as important as Ambrose—we can't tell yet. But it's real, Joan! It's not a dream, or a nightmare, and I'm not a scrap feverish. There really is something! May I fetch the biscuits and then come to your room and tell you all about it?"

Joan looked at her helplessly. "Can't you wait till the morning?"

"No, Joan, darling, I really can't. I should go right off my head if I had to wait, and I couldn't sleep a wink. It's a long time till seven o'clock! Let me tell you, Joan, dear!"

"Very well. But you must do it quickly. I wanted you to have a good night's rest."

"This is better for me than two good nights' rest!" Jen proclaimed in triumph. "You go back to bed and I'll bring the biscuits."

"Joan Shirley, what are you doing down there?" Janice leaned on the gallery rail and stared at them. "A midnight conference?"

"Stars! We've wakened Jandy Mac! More biscuits needed!" Jen chuckled. "It's all right, Jandy, I'm the villain of the night. Joan's trying to send me back to bed, but I'm not going—not yet. She'll tell you! It's the Curate's fault; he tripped me up." She carefully avoided the slim black cat, who had recovered from his fright and was coming to investigate, and ran off to the larder.

"Curate! Come with me, or you'll trip her up again!" Joan tucked him under one arm and held up her long gown in the other hand, as she went upstairs.

Janice eyed her severely. "Such a way to go on, because your mother is in Bournemouth! If you were Joy, I shouldn't be in the least surprised, but for Joan——! Did you tell me you were going to be grown up at Christmas?"

Joan laughed and carried the cat into her room. "There! You've been enough bother for one night. Sit down and tramp on the bed, and presently you shall have some biscuit, if Jen brings the sort you like. Jandy, dear, I'm awfully sorry you've been disturbed. I apologise, but it wasn't my fault. I heard a sound and went to see, and I found Jen sitting at the foot of the stair, having fallen over the Curate. She said she was hungry and wanted a biscuit. I tried to send her back to bed, but she's in a terribly excited state about some idea that has just occurred to her, and she's sure she can't sleep till she's told us. She even said that if I wouldn't listen she would go and tell you. I felt it would be better to let her get it off her mind. Nothing else will satisfy her."

"Has she been having bad dreams?"

"She says no, and that it's really important. You know, the last time she scared me like this it quite truly was a big thing; she wanted to tell me she had found Ambrose's grave down in the tunnels. She reminded me of that, and said this was important too."

"What can she have got hold of this time?"

"I haven't the slightest idea, but she's thrilled to the limit. I'm certain she won't sleep till she has told us."

"Then I'm going to hear what it is, too, and biscuits will certainly be a good idea." Janice stifled a yawn. "I suppose I may perch on your bed beside the Curate? You wouldn't ask me to sit in a chair at this time of night? What time is it, by the way? I didn't stop to look. I came rushing out to see if you'd caught a burglar."

"I'm terribly sorry! It's nearly half-past two. Yes, isn't it scandalous? I'm glad mother and Joy

aren't here. Make yourself at home! We can have
late breakfast, to make up for it. What is that
infant doing downstairs?"

"Oh, no, we can't!" Jen cried from the doorway. "No late breakfasts for any of us! We've
work to do to-morrow. I'll tell you in just two
minutes. Hop into bed, Joan! I'll put this on your
knee."

"What have you brought, Jen?" Joan asked
indignantly.

"Only apples and bread and butter and biscuits,
and a jug of milk and three glasses. There's
nothing nicer than one of your—of Joy's—lovely
apples with bread and butter and milk. But it
meant knives and plates. I like to peel my apples.
There, Jandy Mac! It was to be just biscuits to
keep Joan and me alive, but when you appeared it
turned into a feast."

"Very kind of you, I'm sure. A really thoughtful burglar," Janice mocked.

"Did you think I was a burglar?" Jen grinned.
"It's much more exciting than that! Here, Curate!
I guessed Joan would capture you and bring you
to the feast. Here are water biscuits for you."
And she crumbled some pieces on the edge of the
tray and gave him milk in a saucer.

She handed a plate and knife to Janice. "We'll
all have to wash, but it isn't far to the bathroom.
Is there anything you'd rather have? There's a
very tempting pie in the larder, but I didn't think
you'd fancy it at night."

"Jen!" Joan said sternly. "You're trying to turn this into a midnight feast!"

"Yes, Joan, dear, a feast of rejoicing. But not midnight; we're long past that. You don't mind, do you? Shall I peel your apple for you?"

"She does look over-excited." Janice studied Jen's eager face critically. "We'd better find that ice for her head."

"I *am* over-excited—terribly! And so will you be, when I tell you what it's all about," Jen exulted. "You won't kick and spill that milk, will you, Joan?"

"Jen Robins, tell us what you mean!" Joan said sternly.

Jen looked round at them—at Joan in bed, Janice crouching beside her, the Curate unconscious of anything but milk.

"Well, Joan, I've solved our problem. I've found the field and the V-shaped place and the tree," she said simply. "Wouldn't you be excited if you'd done that, Joan, dear?"

CHAPTER XXII

JEN'S GREAT IDEA

THEY GAZED at one another—Janice in her crimson gown, Joan in her blue one, staring at Jen, whose yellow plaits were in wild disorder.

"Where is it?" Joan asked breathlessly.

"If you really have made a discovery, we'll forgive you for all this disturbance in the small hours," Janice said.

"But how, Jen? How did you find out? And where is the place?" Joan pleaded.

"I can't be certain till we've dug for the treasure and proved it. But I'm sure in my own mind. It's just the place the highwayman would choose. Much more likely than a field away at King's Bottom! And the best of it is"—and Jen hugged herself in glee—"that old Jaikes pig will spend all night digging in the wrong place for something that isn't there and never was there!"

"Tell us where you think it is, Jen." Joan spoke quietly, but with the authority of a senior and a Queen.

Jen responded instantly. "In the gate-house meadow, Joan, dear."

"*What?*" There was a shout from Joan and Janice.

"That's how I felt when I woke up knowing

we'd been all wrong to go to King's Bottom Farm." Jen hurriedly steadied the tray. "It's all right. You only spilt a drop or two. I was prepared; I knew you'd jump."

"Our own meadow!" Joan exclaimed, looking dazed. "The fish-stream and the road through the gate-house—they do meet at the little bridge. It might be, Jen."

"I'm sure it is. They make a V, just the shape that's on the map."

"And the shaded thing, like a building, on the line of the road, is the gate-house itself," Janice cried.

"Yes, Jandy Mac. The road goes right through it. And the cross on the map?" Jen paused expectantly.

"Our tree! Ambrose's tree!" Joan and Janice cried together.

"And we're going to dig round it for the treasure to-morrow, while Mr. Jaikes digs round his tree in the dark to-night! He's doing it at this moment, and not finding anything!" Jen exulted again. "I am so glad about that!"

The elder girls looked at one another. "I shouldn't wonder if she's right, Jandy," said Joan.

"I know I'm right. I woke up knowing. I had a sure and certain feeling I was right. Something inside told me," Jen insisted.

"We were rather dense not to think of it before. It's so very obvious, once it has been pointed out to us," Janice said ruefully.

"Oh, I don't know! It never occurred to Joy."

"Joy never thought that the mysterious map was a place right on her own doorstep," Jen grinned. "You'll let us dig up the meadow, won't you, Joan? You won't be a pig like Mr. Jaikes?"

"If it was the garth, I might hesitate," Joan retorted. "But I've no holy feeling about the meadow. We'll certainly dig—or find somebody to dig for us. But we may not find anything. In that case, we'll have to look for a third V-shaped place."

"There isn't another. We won't need to look any more," Jen said confidently. "Oh, don't you wonder what the treasure is?"

Joan slowly peeled her apple, looking thoughtful. "The Abbey was a heap of ruins, all cluttered up with farm ploughs and carts, with hay stored in the day-room and apples in the chapter-house. Little Jane wandered in and made her play-place in a corner and kept it a secret. Then she had to tell her mother, who was getting anxious about the father's doings; she may not have known he was robbing ladies in their coaches up on the hills, but she probably suspected it. She guessed he might need a hiding-place, so she encouraged Jane and gave her more things for the secret house, and Jane played there and made a fire and fetched water from the stream and did a little cooking. Old Miles discovered the tunnels under the Abbey and used them as a store for his booty; then one day he found the way through the old chest, and it closed after him, and he thought he was buried alive and would never get out again."

Jen shivered. "I thought that about you and Joy and Jandy. I don't really like this story, Joan."

Joan cut her apple into slices and went on: "He dug himself out, but he dropped the wallet that held the rings and brooches and the pearls, and he'd had such a fright that he never went back to find them; he couldn't bear the thought of the tunnels. He came out through the gate-house, as we did. Perhaps it was then he buried something under the tree and made the map; he may have found something down there, or held on to something when he dropped the wallet. Then the police or soldiers, or whoever they were, came after him, and Mrs. Miles said he'd have to get out of the country, and told him——"

"And she cried," Jen interrupted. "She cried and cried, and I don't blame her. She didn't want him to be hanged. Sorry, Joan, dear! I didn't mean to spoil the story."

"She told him about Jane's secret place, and he went there and hid till it was dark, and then he escaped. I don't suppose they ever saw him again. He gave Jane the map and told her to dig there and she'd find something that would bring her luck. It may have been money or jewels, or it may have been some country charm in which he had faith. That's the story, as we know it."

"So far," Janice added. "The next thing is to dig. Perhaps we'll find an old horse-shoe."

"For luck," Jen remarked. "If we do, we'll hang it up in the gate-house, to bring luck to our visitors."

Joan shook her head at her. "The Latin words over the door are more likely to bring them luck than a horse-shoe."

Jen quoted the motto she loved: "'Gate open be To honest men all free.' Yes, it's better than a charm. I wonder if it is just a horse-shoe!"

"Now, don't you go guessing!" Janice said. "You guessed old hymn-books, you know."

"And I got little Jane's diary—much better than I'd guessed!" Jen said in triumph. "I shall hope for a lucky horse-shoe, and perhaps I'll get something simply marvellous."

Joan laughed. "Jenny-Wren, I've forgiven you for your excitement. I don't blame you for being thrilled; you've thrilled us too."

"She certainly couldn't wait till the morning," Janice agreed, helping herself to a biscuit. "I'm glad she provided the feast. We'd have had to go and look for food, after all this chatter."

Jen bowed graciously. "I thought you'd be pleased. At least, I hoped you would. Oh, Joan, couldn't we dress at once and go out and dig?"

"And give Ann and Boniface the shock of their lives? Not likely! You're going back to bed, my dear—unless you'd care to share my bed for the rest of the night?"

"Good idea," Janice remarked. "You can keep tight hold of her, to make sure she doesn't go off and dig on her own. She's quite capable of it."

"I wouldn't leave Joan out. I don't care quite so much about you, Jandy Mac," Jen retorted. "Oh, Joan, let me sleep with you! I'm sure you'd be a soothing influence, and I feel I need it to-night."

"I'll say you do! You'd better stay. But I warn you I'm not going to talk."

"No, Joan. We'll keep quiet," Jen promised.

"I shall fetch Bob, who dug up Lady Jehane's jewels for us," Joan decided. "He's working for our gardener. He's a good lad; he'll keep quiet if we find anything we don't want talked about. Now, Jen and Jandy, pack up the remains of the feast. We shall have to explain to cook in the morning."

"My feast of rejoicing." Jen began to fill the tray.

"Couldn't we wash up and leave no traces of our—our nocturnal adventures?" Janice asked.

"That's a good way to put it, since we can't say midnight feast! I'm not going to wash up to-night!"

"This morning!" Jen put in.

"You're altogether too bright for three a.m., Jenny-Wren; this morning it is. I'll wash up after breakfast, if Susie Spindle hasn't done it for us by then. Now don't drop that tray! I shall carry the Curate, so that you won't trip over him again."

"Oh, couldn't he stay? He's curled round into such a tight little bunch and he's so hot and happy!" Jen pleaded.

"He can't stay, if you do. Three in a bed is one too many. Besides, he'll want to do some more roaming about in half an hour. He'd disturb us just as we were going to sleep. I've had him on my bed before; I know his little ways." And Joan gathered the warm, singing Curate into her arms. "He wouldn't stay; he's far too hot. Lead the way and switch on the lights, Jen. Jandy will carry the tray."

"We're a triumphal procession. Couldn't we sing something? A hymn, perhaps?" Jen suggested.

Janice grinned. "What was that one you spoke of, out of your old book? Something about 'lower lights'? Most appropriate!"

Jen giggled. "'Let the Lower Lights be Burning'! I'll switch on for you, Jandy Mac! I think we won't sing; it might terrify Susie. Joan and the Curate could dance the Helston Furry, in front of you and the tray, and I'll do a jig behind you."

"Stop talking nonsense!" Joan commanded. "Go on, you two. I want to get to bed, and the Curate wants to go out for a ramble."

"I *am* looking forward to to-morrow morning!" Jen sighed happily.

"You mean this morning. Caught you out that time, Jenny-Wren!" Janice exclaimed.

Jen grinned. "Right you are, Jandy Mac! Don't you wonder if it's an old rusty horse-shoe?"

"Or a tiara, or a diamond necklace. Or a hymn-book," Janice teased.

"You won't mind if I don't go to sleep, will you, Joan, dear?" Jen pleaded.

"I'll mind very much. I'm terribly sleepy. You couldn't be so unkind as to keep me awake."

"I won't! Oh, I won't! I'll lie like a mouse when the Mother Superior's watching its hole!"

"I think you'll sleep," Joan said grimly. "You're tired out."

CHAPTER XXIII

DIGGING FOR TREASURE

"I've been to sleep!" Jen sat up, blinking in the sunshine, and stared at Joan, who was brushing her hair.

"You've slept for hours. Look at the time!"

"Nine o'clock! What will cookie think of us?"

"We'll have to own up," Joan remarked.

"I'd better get dressed. We've a lot to do to-day. I say, Joan, what will you do with all that stuff when you put it up at Christmas? I want to know how you're going to look."

Joan glanced at her and hesitated. Then she laughed and quickly twisted her hair into two thick plaits. She swung them round her head and made them safe with hairpins. Then she looked at Jen. "How's that?"

"A crown! Oh, lovely! You look quite grown-up and just terribly pretty. Don't take it down for a moment! Jandy! Hi, Jandy Mac! Come here!" And she ran to the door.

"Oh, Jen! I never said you might call Jandy! It was only for you," Joan protested.

"Jandy'll want to see you. She won't be here at Christmas. She ought to know what you're going to look like."

"What's all this?" Janice came to the door in her crimson gown. "Are you playing charades? Dressing-up? Oh, Joan, you do look pretty! You'll wear it like that when you put it up for good, won't you?"

"That's the idea," Joan explained. "This infant wanted to know how I'd look grown-up. Then she said, quite truly, that you wouldn't be here at Christmas. I've been trying different ways; that's why I had pins ready. What about it, Jandy? Will it do?"

"Beautifully. I should stick to that way; it suits you. I shan't have any bother with mine. I wonder what Jenny-Wren will do with all that mane?"

"Oh, mine's coming off!" Jen said airily. "I shan't have time for hair when I've ten children to look after. I'm going to have it short, like yours. I only keep it long just now to please Father. When it has to go up he won't mind; I dare say he'll be pleased if I cut it off and look like a little girl."

"You won't look like a very little girl if you go on growing at your present rate," Janice mocked. "You'll be a lamp-post or a maypole."

"I like maypole best," Jen said haughtily.

"It's very pretty, Joan, and you look very nice; most impressive! Couldn't you keep it up?"

"Not until I really must." Joan pulled out the pins. "I shall be eighteen soon, and then I suppose it will be necessary. I'm glad to have your approval. Now I won't need to send you a photo!"

"I'd like the photo, all the same. There's the post! I'll fetch the letters. Aren't we naughty girls, to be so late?" And Janice ran downstairs.

They heard her explanation to the maid. "Thanks, I'll take them. We're nearly ready."

"You'd better make that remark true, by starting to get dressed," Joan said severely to Jen. "I'm nearly ready, and Jandy's nearly ready, but you certainly aren't."

"Is there one for me, Jandy Mac?" Jen cried wistfully. "I want to know about father."

"None for you and none for me. Two for Joan."

"You can't expect your mother to write every day, Jenny-Wren," Joan said gently. "And Jandy can't expect to hear from Alec every day, either. Mine are from mother and Joy; Joy said she'd write. Hers will be full of Farmer Jaikes's field and the spot where we're to dig."

Jen chuckled in delight, forgetting her disappointment, as Joan had intended that she should. "And we're going to dig in the gate-house meadow! Oh, be quick, everybody, and let's have breakfast!"

"I like that!" Janice protested. "And you still in your pyjamas and your hair the most ghastly mess! You haven't even been to the bathroom yet. Now Joan and I look almost beautiful enough to go down. There'll be no bacon left by the time you're ready; you'll have to be content with porridge. Shoo! Go and have your bath!"

Jen fled. "I'll ask Susie to do me two eggs, if you greedies eat all the bacon!"

"Joy's full of ideas about our map," Joan said, as they sat down to breakfast. "But, thanks to our early-morning conference, it's all entirely and absolutely out of date."

"Thanks to my bright idea," Jen corrected her. "You do think I'm right, don't you, Joan?"

"I think we shall know quite soon. I've sent a message asking Bob to come along to the gatehouse at ten o'clock. Let me point out that it would have been nine-thirty, if we hadn't slept till nine. That's what comes of meals at three in the morning."

"I had to tell you!" Jen protested.

"She'd have exploded if she hadn't told somebody, with an idea like that inside her," Janice remarked.

"Yes, she had to tell us. But don't be too much upset if we don't find anything, will you, Jen? Whatever it was has been buried for a hundred years or more. It may have rotted or fallen to pieces."

"But the highwayman would wrap it up!" Jen objected.

"That might not save it. And he might not be very careful; he never supposed it would lie there for a century. He gave little Jane the map and expected her to find it."

"It's a pity he didn't explain his map to her!"

Joan looked at her. "Perhaps he did. Perhaps she found the thing, whatever it was, and took it away."

"Oh, Joan!" Jen wailed. "How can you be so blighting!"

"It's only common sense. I don't want you to be too much upset if there's nothing there."

"I shall be fearfully upset! I know we're going to find it!"

"But didn't Jane say she couldn't understand the map?" Janice interposed. "That doesn't sound as if——"

"She did! She did say it! Oh, thank you, Jandy Mac! She said she didn't know what it meant, so she can't have found the place! There, Joan! Now do stop giving me gentle hints and warnings!"

Joan laughed. "Well, if we find nothing, remember how much we have discovered—or rather, have been given. The book for Baby Kat, and the pictures and stories about dear old Ambrose and the Small Ones, and——"

"Minette and her baby and l'ecureuil." Jen gloated over the new word. "And the story of Jane and her play-house. All right, Joan, I'll remember. We haven't done so badly! But, all the same, I hope there's one thing more."

"Greedy! Never satisfied!" Janice mocked.

Half an hour later they went through the

Abbey on their way to the meadow, laden with trowels and spades, for Jen flatly declined to leave all the digging to Bob.

"You can do as you like, but I'm going to help. Perhaps I'll be the one to find the treasure," she said sturdily. "It was a big tree, and we may have to dig all round before we find the thing. It may take a long time."

"I wonder if the roots have grown over the treasure?" Janice began. "It wasn't such a big tree when it was buried."

"It would be fairly big," Joan argued. "The burying wasn't under Ambrose's thin little tree of three hundred years ago. It would have grown a good deal by the highwayman's day."

"Yes, that's true. I was thinking of the small tree in the book of pictures."

"It must have been a fairly hefty tree by Old Miles's time," Joan said.

"Here comes Boniface!" Jen groaned. "Don't let him stop us, Joan, dear! He'll want to talk! Oh, why did we let him live in the Abbey?"

Joan laughed under her breath. "So you're beginning to realise he may sometimes be in the way, Jenny-Wren!—Boniface, we're in a hurry. Don't stop us just now," she said firmly.

Astonished, he stood aside and watched them go out to the meadow, staring after them open-mouthed.

"He thinks we're mad," Janice said.

"We'll tell him afterwards," Jen cried. "We

couldn't possibly stop to gossip now. Oh, there's Bob! Have you told him, Joan?"

"I only told him that we wanted him, and he must bring a spade." Joan went forward to the lad. "Bob, we've found an old paper that makes us think somebody buried something under this tree a long while ago. We don't know what it was or exactly where he put it, but we believe it was under this big tree. Will you help us to dig for it?"

Bob's eyes were round. "Sure, Miss Joan! Will it be jools, like we found in the old church down there?"

"We don't know what it will be, or how deep," Joan confessed. "It might be jewels, or money, or something quite different."

"We think it may have been a horse-shoe," Jen put in.

"A horse-shoe!" Bob's eyes were rounder than ever.

"All we know is that it was to bring somebody luck. That's why we thought of a horse-shoe. It may be some sort of charm," Joan explained. "Where will you start? We'll dig too, but I don't expect we'll go as deep as you will."

"We'll start, and if we don't find anything, Bob can come and dig our holes deeper still." Jen was tremulous with excitement.

Joan glanced at her. "I've a good mind to send you home to bed. You're all shaky with thrills."

"She ought to be lying down in the dark, with ice on her head."

"Stop talking about putting ice on my head!" Jen raged. "Go and put your own head under a cold tap, Jandy Mac! Why don't we start?"

"Bob has started," Joan pointed out. "Get to work, everybody! And try to keep cool, Jen, dear."

"Cool! I'm thrilled to the limit," Jen muttered.

"You are. That's the trouble," Janice told her.

"Well, at least I'm going to do something useful and not just talk!" And Jen attacked the ground at the side of the tree farthest from where Bob was digging stolidly.

Joan and Janice chose their spots, avoiding the roots of the big elm and working between them. There was silence, as everyone dug steadily.

For a long time there was no result. The girls paused to rest occasionally; Bob dug deeply, but found nothing.

"We're making a fearful mess of the meadow," Janice said.

"We'll easily put that right. But I'm beginning to feel rather hopeless. It will be a blow if we find nothing, after all this work," Joan admitted.

"I hope no tourists come this morning." Jen leaned on her spade and surveyed the heaps of earth. "They'd think we were quite mad. The owner of the Abbey tearing her meadow to pieces!"

"They might offer to help," Janice suggested.

"We don't want them," Jen said hurriedly. "We don't want outsiders butting in. I say, doesn't Bob dig beautifully? I wish I could do it like that!"

Bob grinned and worked on.

"I hope he'll be the one to find it," Jen added loudly. "He's done all the really useful digging. We only scratch off the top layer. He'd be so pleased if he found something simply marvellous."

"Or an old horse-shoe," Janice laughed.

Bob's grin deepened, but he did not speak.

"Come on! We'll have another try!" And Jen made a fresh onslaught on the hard ground.

Suddenly Bob gave a cry. "Something here, Miss Joan!"

The girls flung down their spades and ran to him.

"Oh, Bob, what is it? What have you found? Show us!" Jen shouted.

"I ain't dug her out yet, but spade struck something hard." And Bob jumped down into his hole and began to scrape away the soil. "Gimme that trowel, little Miss Jen."

"I bet it's only a big stone," Janice murmured.

Jen ran for the trowel which Joan had been using. She let "little Miss Jen" pass in the excitement of the moment, but stored it up for indignant comment later on.

"Here's a box o' some sort," said Bob.

"A box! Then it *is* the treasure!" A look flashed among the girls.

Very carefully Bob drew out a small metal box, rusted and discoloured, but whole.

"Her ain't broke." And he handed it up to Joan. "Will it be that would bring luck, think ye?"

"What's inside it, perhaps." Joan's hands shook a little as she took the box, while Jen and Janice pressed closely on her to see.

CHAPTER XXIV

BROWN BEADS

A SQUARE of tarpaulin, neatly folded, filled the small box, which Bob, at Joan's command, broke open. Holding their breath, Jen and Janice watched her lift the cloth.

"Carefully wrapped up, after all," Joan murmured.

"Oh, Joan! What's in it, Joan?" Jen whispered.

Joan drew the folds of cloth aside. "Look, girls!"

"Beads!" Janice cried, astounded. "They don't look valuable or lucky!"

"Only old brown wooden beads!" Jen wailed. "They're not worth finding!"

"Don't be in such a hurry," Joan said quietly. She lifted the beads and showed that they were strung together on a silver chain. "Now do you see?" she asked reverently.

"A necklace! But why would it bring luck to Jane?" Janice asked, bewildered.

"Brown beads!" Jen said slowly. "You said something about brown beads, not long ago. What was it, Joan?"

"Think!" Joan commanded, with a quick look at her, full of meaning. "What did I say about brown beads?"

"You're holding them as if they were made of gold or diamonds," Janice observed. "Why do they matter so much?"

"Joan! Oh, Joan, did they belong to Ambrose?" Jen cried. "Is it his—what did you call it—the thing we think the squirrel stole?"

"Ambrose's rosary. Of course it is! It may not be gold or diamonds, Jandy Mac, but it's a great treasure, all the same."

"Ambrose used it when he said his prayers!" Jen's voice was awed. "Oh, Joan, it is a treasure! What a lovely thing to find!"

"Ambrose used it every day, and many times a day. I expect he had it for years." Joan looked up at the staring Bob. "You know about old Ambrose, the monk who lived here, Bob? This is a prayer-chain—the one he used when he prayed."

"Well, now, to think o' that!" Bob appreciated their excitement over the discovery, even if to him it seemed exaggerated. "Him's the old one what's buried down in the tunnels, where the big chest is, Miss Joan?"

"Yes, Bob. He lived in the gate-house, and he used to sit under this tree that we've had to cut down. I expect he said his prayers there many a time."

"He had a little striped cat called Minette, and a squirrel called l'ecureuil," Jen said breathlessly. "Joan, do you really think l'ecureuil stole the rosary?"

"I expect the squirrel took it and poked it into some hole in the rubbish that lay about everywhere. Ambrose searched for it but never found it, and Katharine and Peregrine gave him a new one. It ought to have a crucifix hanging from it, but that must have been lost during its adventures. Perhaps the squirrel or the highwayman was rough!"

"And when Old Miles was trapped in the tunnels, two hundred years later, and had to fight his way out, he uncovered it," Janice added. "He saw what it was and he clutched it, hoping it would help him to find his way through the mess he was in. He'd be sure to be superstitious, and we've always believed he had the fright of his life down there."

"If he hadn't been so terrified, he'd have gone back to look for his wallet, with the rings and pearls in it, which we found," Jen added.

"He can't have gone back—or if he did, he couldn't find the wallet," Joan said. "He made those maps, which Jandy brought to us last June, and he left them with his son, who carried on at the farm. They were handed down in the family, but no one knew what to make of them; then John Miles, the great-grandson, gave them to Joy's and Jandy's Uncle Tony, and Jandy inherited them and brought them to us. But the highwayman buried the rosary separately; I think perhaps he found his way out of the tunnel after—just after—he had picked it up, and he felt it had brought him luck. He buried it here, outside the gate-house, and he thought he gave his little girl a clue, so that she would find it. But she wasn't clever enough to read it, so she kept it inside her diary, and no one knew it was there till Vinny Miles found it and showed it to us."

"A squirrel — and a highwayman — and Lavinia! And now we have the rosary!" Janice said. "So that's why he told Jane it would bring her luck! It's better than a horse-shoe!"

"It's the most lovely find we could have had! Let me hold it, Joan!" Jen pleaded.

She took the chain reverently and looked carefully at the beads. "They're carved into patterns. Even if we didn't know what it is, it's jolly pretty. What will you do with it?"

"What do you think? You certainly ought to have some say in the matter. It's owing to you we have the rosary, because Lavinia gave her book to you."

"Didn't Jen have Ambrose's gold ring?" Janice asked.

Jen looked at her quickly. "I still feel I ought not to have it, but it is my very dearest treasure."

"Would you like to have his rosary too? After Mother and Joy have seen it, of course," Joan began.

Jen reddened. "No, Joan, dear. It's terribly kind of you, but I wouldn't dream of it. Ambrose's beads must stay in the Abbey, with the books that tell us all about him, and about Jane and her father, and Katharine and Peregrine. The whole story's there, for anyone who cares to put it together. The rosary must stay there too."

"Good for you, Jen! I do agree!" Janice exclaimed.

"Yes, Jen is right," Joan said. "The rosary shall lie in the refectory beside the books."

"Perhaps it will bring luck to the Abbey! At any rate, it will bring me, for I shall want to come to see it often," Jen declared.

"You'll be very welcome." Joan smiled at her. "We're always glad to see you."

"It didn't bring luck to Jane; but then, she never found it," Jen went on. "We've found it! Do you think perhaps——?"

"No, I don't," Joan said firmly. "I don't believe in things that bring luck. But I'd say that the rosary has brought us something already, in the happy feeling we have because we've found it."

"And because it helps to make old Ambrose even more real to us," Janice added.

"Thank you for your help, Bob." Joan looked at the tall lad. "The beads will mean something to you, anyway, for I shall give you a present because you've worked so hard for us."

"Thank ye, Miss Joan. I'll allus come when you wants me to dig. Shall I put this here muck back and make the place neat again?"

"Thank you very much; yes, please do! I don't suppose we shall want anything more dug up," Joan said with a laugh. "But we'll certainly ask you, if we do."

They went through the Abbey, seeing nothing of Ann or Boniface, Joan carrying the box with the rosary.

"We'll keep this in the house till Mother and Joy have seen it," she said.

As they reached the terrace Jen dashed ahead to the hall table, where lay the letters which had come by the second post.

"One for Jandy. One for me. Joan had hers this morning. Mine's from Mother!"

She tore it open, skimmed through the first few lines, and gave a shout. "Father's better, and Mother thinks they can go home in a few days. The rosary has brought me luck, after all! It's the very news I've been hoping for!"

"I am so glad, Jen, dear!" Joan said heartily.

CHAPTER XXV

SUSIE SPINDLE IN TROUBLE

"I'M BOTHERED about one thing, Joan and Jandy," Jen said that evening, as they rested on the lawn after a hectic game of tennis, in which Janice had easily beaten the other two.

"Has the set been too much for you?" Joan looked at her anxiously. "I wasn't sure if we should let you play."

"Not the tennis. It was super! But isn't Jandy Mac a smasher! I can't play her balls at all."

"Australian tennis," Janice said solemnly.

"I can't play them very well myself," Joan admitted. "What's the trouble, Jenny-Wren?"

"It's moral," Jen said seriously, pushing back the plaits from her hot face.

The elder two looked at her in amusement.

"Out with it, then!" Joan commanded. "We know your conscience is very active."

"Jacky-boy says it's terrific. Joan, ought we to keep that rosary? Shouldn't it be Lavinia's? The map was in her book."

"What a conscience!" Janice teased. "Anyone can see the rosary belongs to the Abbey. It's a relic of Ambrose."

"But we only found it because of Vinny!"

"What use would the rosary be to Lavinia, Jen?"

"None at all, of course. But if it's hers, Joan—oughtn't we to do something about it?"

"Who said we wouldn't do something about it?"

"Oh!" Jen's face lit up. "What can we do? Shall we pay her fare to Canada?"

"I'd rather her father and brothers did that. Then we'd feel sure they wanted her."

"I quite agree. It's their job," Janice assented.

Jen eyed Joan closely. "You've some other plan. What is it, Joan?"

"What about clothes? Lavinia ought to have an outfit, to start her on her new life, even if it's just a few things—a new coat and cap for the voyage, a frock or two, and some undies."

"Oh, yes!" Jen cried joyfully. "We'll get them for her! We'll do her shopping! It will be fun! Some red frocks and a red coat, Joan, and a woolly jumper—a bright yellow one! Won't she be pleased?"

"She'll be gay, if you dress her in red and yellow," Janice remarked. "Canada will be able to see Lavinia coming. Don't make her too gaudy! You may scare her folks."

"You'll let me help, won't you, Joan?" Jen pleaded.

"If you're here, of course I shall want your help," Joan assured her gravely. "But won't you have gone home?"

Jen's face fell. "I suppose I shall. I want to see Mother and Father terribly much, but I'd like to be here to help to dress Lavinia. Couldn't we take her shopping before I go?"

"You can't be in two places at once," Janice said.

"I'm afraid we can't, Jen, dear. We must wait till we hear she is to go to Montreal. Her people aren't likely to think of sending a cable; it will take some time for a letter to come."

"Couldn't we cable to them, saying: ' Matter urgent. Please cable reply'?"

"I suppose we could, but we won't," Joan said, laughing. "If they're farm folk it might upset them dreadfully. I'll tell you what we buy for Vinny, Jen. Joy will love to help."

"I shall be jealous of Joy. Perhaps it will take them so long to write that I shall have come back for next term."

"That's much more likely than a cable," Joan agreed. "We must tell Lavinia that we've found out what her map meant."

"And show her the rosary. She won't have an idea what it is," Janice remarked.

"Shall we take it to King's Bottom for her to see it?" Jen suggested. "Couldn't we tell her to come here? We might lose it, or drop it, or something."

"I can't imagine any of us either losing or dropping it! But I'm sure Lavinia would like to come here. I'll ask her to come."

"We could go to-morrow and invite her. Oh no! I forgot. We're taking Jandy Mac to lunch with the President to-morrow."

"It's jolly nice of Cicely to ask me," Janice said.

"She remembers you from that fête last summer, when you were my maid-of-honour for one day. Lavinia could come to-morrow evening. I'll send a note by Susie; she'll like the walk."

When the note was written and Susie was sent for, she did not seem overjoyed, however. She stood looking almost sulky and then burst out: "I don't want to go."

"Why, Susie, whatever is the matter?" Joan exclaimed. "I can send one of the boys, but I thought you'd like the walk."

"That there Vinny Miles comes here too much," Susie muttered.

"Susie, what's wrong with you to-day?" Jen cried, astounded.

Joan raised her eyebrows. "Really, Susie! That's for us to say. We want to see Vinny, and that's enough."

"You always wants her!" Susie was almost in tears.

"Susie's jealous," Janice said suddenly. "I wonder why?"

"Susie, you couldn't be such an ass!" Jen exploded.

"Vinny brings you presents," Susie half-sobbed. "And you was hurt along of her. And you gives her things!" She was struggling for self-control. "I haven't got nothing to give you."

"Come here, Susie," Joan said quietly. "No, don't run away. We didn't know you felt like this. You don't understand. We are trying to arrange for Vinny to go to her father and brothers, away across the sea in Canada. If they'll have her, I don't suppose any of us will ever see her again. Is it worth while making yourself unhappy, when in a few weeks she may have gone?"

Susie dashed her hand across her eyes. "She'll go away?"

"Jen, suppose you take Susie and tell her all about it?" Joan suggested.

"Right! Come on, Susie Spindle! But don't be more of an idiot than you can help," Jen urged. "She'll go to King's Bottom, Joan. Can I go with her?"

"No," Joan said promptly. "You mustn't do too much yet. You'll stay here with Jandy and me. If Susie doesn't want to go, tell me quickly, and I'll find somebody else."

"I will go, Miss Joan," Susie muttered shame-facedly.

"Come on, then! I'll go with you as far as the gate." And Jen seized her arm and pulled her away.

"I had no idea." Joan looked at Janice. "I couldn't scold the poor kid. She's eaten up with jealousy, because we seem to be taking so much notice of Lavinia."

"Why is it?" Janice asked, much intrigued.

"It's because of Jen. Susie worships Jen; so does Lavinia. There was sure to be trouble, but I'll admit I hadn't foreseen it."

"It's quite wise of both the kids. They might do worse than adore Jenny-Wren."

"It won't hurt her; she's too sensible; and it can only do them good. We had trouble with Susie during the measles time. She told me Jen's secret about the pictures of the old church, without understanding what she was doing. Jen was heartbroken with disappointment and furious with Susie. In her excitement—you know what she is?"

Janice grinned.

"I do. She said too much? Did Susie cry herself sick?"

"Just that. Susie was starting measles, though we didn't know. Jen forgave her, but not till Susie's poor little heart had nearly broken too. She's devoted to Jen, who has been very good to Timothy—the brother Susie adores. Now she feels Lavinia has butted in. You can forgive her for being upset."

"Another reason for hoping Lavinia will go to Canada!"

"Yes, but I hope old Boniface will rise to the occasion and go too. I don't like to think of Vinny going alone. The stewardess might not be kind. Vinny would be very lonely."

"They're mostly nice. But of course she might

be unlucky. She'd be much happier if she had her uncle."

Jen came racing back. "Susie's gone. I made her put on decent shoes; she was rushing off in her slippers—on those rough cart roads! I told her not to be silly."

"You can do anything with Susie, Jen," Joan said gently.

Jen reddened. "I know. I'm afraid it's true. Isn't she soft?"

"No, very sensible," Janice told her.

"Be careful what you say to her." Joan made no further comment. "And don't talk to her too much about Lavinia."

"We'd better not tell her about Vinny's new clothes."

Joan laughed. "Much better not. Susie needn't know anything about Lavinia's outfit. The idea will never occur to her."

CHAPTER XXVI

A CALL FOR JEN

"WHAT IS IT?" Lavinia stared at the chain of beads and then at Joan and Jen.

They had explained the map, to her great amazement. Standing in the meadow, they showed her the road through the gate-house, meeting the fish-stream, and the stump of the old tree, just where the cross was marked on the plan.

"We thought at first it was in the Long Meadow, at your farm," Joan added, as they went back to the house.

Lavinia looked at her in sudden understanding. "Did you tell Mr. Jaikes?"

"We had to tell him, because we wanted to dig round his tree. He said no, and then we came home and decided to try our own meadow instead."

"And there we found the treasure," Jen added triumphantly.

Lavinia looked at the beads, as if to her they seemed unworthy of so high a title, as was, indeed, the case. Just some old brown beads! Even if they had been used by a monk hundreds of years ago, she could not feel they were so very precious.

But it was plain that they were important to Miss Joan and Miss Jen, who knew so much more than she did.

"Mr. Jaikes been diggin' round the tree in Long Meadow," she said. "I guess he thinks as how there's somethin' there."

Jen gave a shout of delight. "We hoped he would! Did he dig all night, Vinny?"

"Most o' two nights, I reckon. He were terrible cross these last two mornin's."

Joan laughed. "Poor Mr. Jaikes! But he wasn't nice to us."

"I'm not a bit sorry for him," Janice declared. "I hope he'll spend several more nights digging."

"Oh, no! We must tell him it was a mistake, and that we've found the buried box—on our own ground."

"Don't tell him!" Jen was hugging herself in glee. "Let him go on thinking it's there, and digging without finding anything, till he grows old and grey with disappointment. Serves him right!"

"Certainly not! Don't be spiteful! I'll write a note and explain."

"Don't send it by Lavinia," Janice warned her. "If it annoys him too much, he might turn on her."

"I don't want to take him no letters," Vinny said hurriedly, looking alarmed.

"*Any* letters!" Jen reproved her.

"I'll post the letter," Joan promised.

Susie Spindle appeared at the door. "Miss Joan is wanted on the telephone." She looked doubtfully at Lavinia and went indoors, while Joan ran to take the call.

"I expect it's Joy again," Jen shouted after her. "Perhaps she's had your letter telling how we found the treasure."

"It's too soon for that," Janice objected.

Joan came to the door. "Jen, it's for you. Your mother wants to speak to you."

"Mother? Where is she? Shall I be able to hear her?" Jen leapt to the doorway.

"I heard her all right. She didn't say where she was."

"I hope Father isn't worse." And Jen rushed to the telephone.

"I'm sure he isn't," Joan called after her.

"If it had been bad news, Mrs. Robins would have asked me to break it gently," she said to Janice.

"I expect they want the kid to go home. We shall miss her."

"Vinny, suppose you run off now," Joan suggested.

"Will Miss Jen go away?" Lavinia faltered.

"If her mother wants her, of course she'll go at once. Now don't be silly!" Joan said sternly. "This isn't Jen's home, you know."

"I forgot," Lavinia muttered.

"We all forget," Janice remarked. "Jen seems a

part of the landscape. It's odd to think she lives somewhere else, and has a family we have never seen."

"Off you go, Vinny!" said Joan.

Reluctantly Lavinia turned and went away through the garden.

"She'll weep because she may never see Jen again," Joan said grimly. "But it can't be helped. What a pity girls care so much!"

Jen came flying back, ablaze with excitement. "They want me to go at once. They're home, and Father's stood the journey well, and they want to see me and hear all about everything. How soon can I go, Joan?"

"To-morrow morning. Jandy and I will see that you're ready, won't we, Jandy Mac?"

"I'm a famous packer." Janice pretended to roll up her sleeves. "Let's start! Shall we take her to town and put her in the train in charge of the guard?"

"I can travel alone! I always do!" Jen cried wrathfully.

"In this state of excitement, you might do anything," Janice said. "You'd probably take the wrong train and go to Edinburgh instead of—where is it?"

"Sheffield. We live on the moors, nine hundred feet up, but Sheffield's the station. Mother will meet me; we're to wire when I've started, so that she'll know the time I'll arrive."

"We'll certainly put you into the train," Joan

said. "But I don't think we need trouble the guard."

"And when we've got rid of you, Joan and I will do some trousseau shopping."

"Not for Vinny?" Jen asked anxiously. "We don't know yet that she's to go. I do want to help!"

"No, dear, for me," Janice explained. "I need an outfit too. I may as well do some of my shopping in London."

"Oh! Yes, of course! What fun you'll have! Tell me everything you buy, Jandy Mac. Where's Lavinia? I'd better say good-bye to her."

"I sent her home," Joan said. "If we hear she's going before you come back, you can write to her. But I think very likely she'll still be here. The arrangements may take some time."

"I'd like to see her again before she vanishes into the wilds of Canada," Jen admitted. "You will write and tell me all the plans, won't you? I want to know about dear Boniface, and if his daughter wants him. And what Joy says when she sees Baby Kat's book, and if she likes Minette and the baby and l'ecureuil. You must tell me everything, Joan!"

"I shall make Jandy help. She's a good one for letters. Now let's start on your trunk! It must be all ready to-night. There won't be time to think in the morning."

"And no midnight visiting!" Janice suggested.

"Certainly not. Remember that, Jenny-Wren.

When you go to bed to-night, you stay there."
Jen pouted. "I'd like to come and talk to you."
"I knew it!" Janice grinned.
"I shall lock my door, so it won't be any use,"
Joan said firmly.

CHAPTER XXVII

DOUBTS OF BONIFACE

"Joy! Joy! Are you all right again? Do you like the things we found?"

Jen, brown and well after four weeks on her heather-clad moorland, sprang from the car and hurled herself on Joy, on the terrace before the Hall.

"Don't strangle me! Sorry we couldn't meet you in town, but Cicely turned up unexpectedly and stayed to tea, and we couldn't go off and leave her." Joy, a second Joan, with the same brown eyes and long, dark red hair, struggled out of her wild embrace. "I'm very fit, and I'm thrilled with all your finds. How you could be so clever without me to help, is more than I can imagine!"

"No need to ask how Jenny-Wren is!" Janice strolled out to them. "What a colour! It makes your hair look silly, my dear."

"I always go brown. You should see where I live! I am so glad you're still here! I thought you'd have gone by now."

"They can't get rid of me," Janice laughed.

"I don't expect they want to. Is Joan all right?"

"Not too bad, in spite of a lot of hard work." Joan came to greet her. "You seem to have recovered from that blow on the head!"

"I've forgotten all about it. Where's your mother?" And Jen ran in to find Mrs. Shirley, whom she loved.

"Now tell me everything!" she demanded, as she sat down to the special tea provided for the traveller. "It's jolly nice of you to have me for three days before term begins! Mother and Father didn't mind; they're so glad I've found such nice kind friends near school," she said demurely, her eyes dancing. "I'm glad too. I know I'm very lucky. Oh, Joan, look!" And she ran to her travelling-bag, searched in it, and flourished a cheque. "Ten pounds! Mother sent it to help with Lavinia's outfit. She wanted to have a share in it."

"How very, very kind of Mrs. Robins!" Joan exclaimed, while Joy and Janice and Mrs. Shirley cried out in delight. "I suppose you know why you've come here for the last three days of the holidays?"

"To help to dress Vinny?" Jen said hopefully. "You haven't done it all, have you? I wrote and asked you to wait for me."

"We've waited, but we didn't know you were bringing such a handsome contribution. We've fitted her out with shoes and a trunk and suitcase, but for the really thrilling things we thought we'd like to have your help. To-morrow we four are going to town, with all Lavinia's measurements, to spend money and bring home a regular trousseau."

"Oh, glory! I brought a special present for her —some red beads. She'll love them. I brought some for Susie as well—blue ones," Jen added. "I thought I'd better not leave her out."

"Very wise!" Joan and Janice spoke together.

"What about dear Boniface? Is he getting an outfit too? You told me his daughter wants him to come. Vinny's father is pleased, isn't he? May I see the letters?"

"You may. All the relations have risen to the occasion and have sent money for fares, and Lavinia's father has sent a present to Mrs. Jaikes, to repay her for her care of Vinny, so everybody is happy. Boniface's daughter is thrilled at the thought of seeing her old father again, and Vinny's dad and stepmother want her to come, and will meet her at Montreal when we send the name of the ship and the date she'll arrive."

"Is Vinny pleased?"

"In the seventh heaven of delight. I believe she's even reconciled to the thought of going away from you."

"Thank goodness for that!" Jen said fervently. "We'll put them safely on the ship, won't we? Then it will be easy for them. They do seem such Babes in the Wood to be starting for Canada!"

"I wish we felt as sure of Boniface as we do of Lavinia," Janice remarked.

"Why? What's wrong with him?" Jen cried.

"Jandy thinks the old chap's going to funk at

the last minute," Joy explained. "I hope he won't.
I don't like to feel he's always about when we go
into the Abbey."

"There was a look in his eye I didn't like, last
time we spoke to him about the journey," Janice
said.

"I hope that won't happen." Joan spoke
anxiously. "We can't force him to go, but
everyone would be terribly disappointed if he drew
back now—his daughter and her family, and poor
Vinny."

"And us," Joy said grimly. "We want to get rid
of him out of the Abbey. It will never seem ours
again till he goes."

"I think his son wants him to go." Joan made
no comment on Joy's attitude. "Boniface is
visiting the son and his family, to say good-bye,
Jen. He'll be back to-morrow night."

"Have you booked their passage?"

"Not yet. Jandy's going to make inquiries in
town. The letters only came this week," Joan
explained.

After a hilarious day of shopping in town, the
car brought the four girls home, laden with dress-
boxes and parcels and bundles. A trunk and a
suitcase had been bought in Wycombe and stood
waiting at the farm in Lavinia's tiny room, and
Vinny looked into them and imagined them filled
with new lovely clothes, every night before she
went to bed.

In the privacy of Joan's room the purchases

were shown to Mrs. Shirley. "We don't want Susie to see all these splendours. It would be too hard on her," Joan told her mother. "We'll take them to King's Bottom and help Lavinia to pack. She doesn't know we've been to town, so it won't hurt her to wait a day or two."

"They are good, useful garments." Mrs. Shirley approved their choice. "I was afraid you might not get suitable things."

Jen blushed and looked self-conscious. "If it had been left to me, some of them wouldn't have been very sensible. I wanted different things; but I see now they'd have been just silly."

"We had Joan to keep us straight," Janice laughed. "She was very stern."

"She might have been you yourself." Joy looked at her aunt. "She wouldn't stand any nonsense."

"We couldn't waste dear Mrs. Robins' money," Joan retorted.

"What about booking passages for the travellers?" Mrs. Shirley asked.

"We haven't done it definitely, but Jandy has a list of ships and berths. We only have to write and confirm the dates."

"I want to be sure of old Boniface, before we book his berth," Janice said grimly. "I don't feel too happy about him. Lavinia may have to travel in charge of the stewardess, after all."

"She'd hate that. I hope it won't happen." Joan looked troubled.

"She'd be all right. But it would be jollier for

her to have company. We'd better go to see the old chap after tea."

"Don't let him cry off!" Joy said. "I want him out of the Abbey. I'm not as crazy about the place as Joan and Jen are, but I do like to feel it belongs to us after closing time, and that we can go in there to be quiet, without thinking an ancient spectre may appear in a doorway at any moment."

"Joy, he's not that!" Jen cried.

"He hasn't been any trouble. He never interrupts or is a nuisance," Joan said.

"No, but he's always there. I know you meant to be kind, but I'm sure it was a mistake. Now that we've this chance to get rid of him, we mustn't let it slip," Joy insisted. "Send him off to Canada! That's what I say."

"Don't come with us, when we go to see him, if that's how you feel," Joan said urgently. "I'd hate him to know anyone thinks he's a nuisance. It would break his heart."

"I'm not coming. He hasn't had much to do with me. You three are his pals; you'll do the job better than I should." Joy thrust the task on to the others. "But don't let him back out now. He can't be allowed to let everybody down."

"I hope his son has eased his mind, so that he won't be so frightened. I believe he's terrified of the journey," Joan suggested.

"Well, poor dear, can you wonder?" Jen

exclaimed. "I don't suppose he's ever seen a ship! I'd be scared myself."

"He hasn't seen the sea, or a ship, except in pictures. He told us so," Joan said. "But we can make it so easy for him! He really hasn't anything to be afraid of."

"If we can only make him believe that!" Janice said doubtfully.

CHAPTER XXVIII

SUSIE IS SENSIBLE

"Miss Jen! Oh, please, Miss Jen!" Susie Spindle caught Jen as she went downstairs.

"What's the matter, Susie? Anything I can do?"

"Let me see them things you bought for Vinny! Oh, please, Miss Jen!"

Jen stood, one hand on the banister rail, and stared down at her. "Who told you we had bought things for Vinny? We thought you wouldn't like to know."

"Vinny told me you said you'd get things for her to go to America in. I saw her in the village. You had parcels in the car and you been to London."

"I see. I'll ask Joan." And Jen went thoughtfully on her way.

"We'd better let her see the clothes, Joan," she urged, as they went through the garden to find Boniface. "I don't believe it will upset her; she sounded quite calm, only interested. It will be a treat for her; she doesn't have too many."

Joan looked troubled. "I don't want to make her more jealous of Lavinia."

"I don't think it will. You can remind her that Vinny's going away, for good and all."

"Perhaps Susie's developing some sense," Janice said. "She's older than Lavinia, isn't she?"

"Quite two years. Vinny isn't thirteen yet; Susie is fifteen. I'll speak to her; we could ask Lavinia here and let her and Susie have a private view, if Susie is really going to be sensible."

"That would be fun, and they'd both feel better," Jen said. "Susie doesn't like to feel left out. It's as if we and Vinny had a secret from her."

"I see that," Joan admitted. "I don't want to be unfair to her."

"Here's your old friend," Janice said as Boniface came to meet them on the garth. "And I don't like the look on his face one bit."

Boniface Browning looked old and careworn. As he met the girls he broke into restless, unhappy speech. "Miss Joan! I can't do it! I can't go on the sea, with nobody to help. I'm feared o' that ship! Let me bide here in the quiet!"

"Oh, Boniface, you mustn't back out now!" Joan exclaimed. "Think how disappointed your daughter and her family would be! And think of poor little Vinny!"

"You won't be alone on the ship, my dear man!" Janice urged. "There will be crowds of people to take care of you—the captain, and the sailors, and the stewards! They're always kind."

"They'll tell you what to do," Jen added. "And Jandy will tell you before you start. She's been on heaps of ships."

The old man's frightened eyes turned to Janice. "If you was goin' too, miss——! But I can't go, not alone with just young Vinny. I'm feared! It's too far."

Eagerly the girls told him how easy it would be—the car right to the dockside, the waiting ship, friends ready to help in Montreal.

"And if the sea makes you feel ill, you can just go to bed and stay there," Janice told him. "I've done it many a time. People are very good to you."

But Boniface's nerve had given way. He was nearly in tears as he repeated that he was afraid, that it was too far, that he could not go with only Vinny for company.

Jen pulled Joan's arm. "Come away and leave him to think it over!"

"I thought he was going to cry," she explained, as they went gloomily through the garden. "Then we might have cried too. Oh, Joan—Jandy! Isn't it awful? What are we going to do?"

"It's too much for him," Joan said sombrely. "He doesn't mean to go."

"He needs somebody to hold his hand," Janice remarked. "He can't face it alone."

"It will be worse for Vinny, if she has to go alone," Jen urged.

"The tragedy is that he really wants to go. He's pining to see his daughter and the great-grandchildren," Joan groaned. "I know that's true, by the way he spoke before. But he can't face the journey. It's too big an effort at his age."

"Such an easy journey!" Janice insisted.

"But we can't make him believe it," Joan said, in despair.

"Wait a day or two. He may think better of it. But we ought to book the berths."

"I know, Jandy. But we can't book for an old man who won't go."

"Oh, he must go! We can't give up hope! Think of Vinny!" Jen wailed. "That poor kid! She couldn't bear it, if she had to go quite alone!"

"Don't suggest it to her, so long as there's any chance," Joan advised. "We'll try to buck Boniface up, for Vinny's sake. And we'll let Susie fetch her to-morrow to see her new clothes. It will make the journey seem real to Lavinia. I don't think she quite believes in it yet."

She spoke to Susie that evening. "You know we are giving Vinny Miles new clothes for her trip to Canada?"

Susie looked back at her frankly. "Yes, Miss Joan. She's glad. She hadn't no—she hadn't any things to go in."

"No, she needed a big coat and some other clothes. Would you like to see them?"

Susie's eyes sparkled. "I would that! You give—you gave me lots of new things when I came here," she added.

"So we did. You hadn't very much, had you?"

"You gave me pretty prints and aprons for

mornings and a good black dress, but they was for my work. 'Sides those, you give me a lovely blue frock to wear on my days out," Susie said breathlessly, her careful English beginning to desert her in her eagerness. "There wa'n't no call for you to do that. It was just to be kind. I don't never forget that blue frock, Miss Joan."

Joan's eyes were bright. "Susie, how very nice of you! You look so jolly in that frock when you go to the village. You won't feel sore if we give Vinny a few things, when she needs them so badly, will you?"

"Vinny's going away, from everybody, and from you and Miss Jen. I wouldn' like that." Susie's experience told her that Jen would be at the Hall constantly, for week-ends and extra days, even though her home might be somewhere mysteriously called "the North" or "moors". "I'd rather stay here than have lots of new frocks."

"Oh, I see! You're being very sensible, Susie. But don't forget that Vinny is going to her father and her family; she wants to go. Don't say anything to frighten her or make her feel it's a long way."

"No, Miss Joan. And she'll go with her old uncle. But I ain't got no uncles or fathers or families. I'll stay here always, won't I?"

"That will depend on yourself," Joan said cheerfully. "So long as cook is satisfied with you, you'll certainly stay, if you want to."

"I'd like to be cook some day."

"There's no reason at all why you shouldn't be a cook. Learn all you can, and when the time comes we'll see. To-morrow you can put on the blue frock and go and fetch Vinny to see her new clothes. Tell cook you are to have a holiday."

Much cheered, Susie went back to her duties. And still more cheered, Joan went to the other girls and told them of the interview.

"Susie being sensible at last!" Joy mocked. "She's growing up. She really has been rather a baby for her age."

"How lovely of her to say that about the blue frock! To understand and appreciate it, I mean!" Jen cried. "I like Susie a lot better than I did!"

"Joan, Jen and I went back to see old Boniface, as you suggested," Janice said. "I thought I might be able to convince him that the journey would be easy. But it wasn't any use. He almost wept again and kept saying he couldn't go alone, and Vinny was too young to be any good. He feels he'll need to take care of her, and he wants to be taken care of himself."

"He kept on saying, 'If only somebody else could go, somebody what knows about ships'," Jen groaned. "We can't go to Canada, just to hold his hand!"

"Let me talk to him!" Joy suggested. "I'll soon get rid of him for you!"

"How would you do that?" Joan demanded.

"Tell him flatly that he isn't wanted in the

Abbey any longer and he'd better go to his own people, who do want him."

"Joy! You couldn't! You'd break his heart!" Jen wailed.

"You mustn't do it, Joy. I won't have it," Joan said quickly. "The Abbey is mine, and I've said he may stay. I won't have him driven out."

"It would be all for his good," Joy argued. "He'd be glad, once he'd started."

"I dare say he would, but I won't have him frightened. I'm beginning to be afraid it's too late and he really is too old for such a great effort."

"But what about Vinny?" Jen said urgently. "She'll break her heart if she has to go alone. It would be terribly hard on her!"

"I don't know, and that's the truth," Joan admitted. "I feel rather hopeless. If only Boniface would be sensible, like Susie Spindle!"

And in the lowest possible spirits, on this one point, the girls looked at one another, but found no new suggestion and no way to help.

CHAPTER XXIX

THE BABES IN THE WOOD ARE AFRAID

"Oh, Miss Joan! Be these all for me?" Lavinia's breath was taken away by the display in Joan's room.

Mrs. Shirley was installed in a corner to watch. Susie, in her pretty blue frock, had fetched Lavinia, and the two had come racing in delight to see the dress parade, as Joy called it. But now Vinny, gazing enthralled at her new possessions, was almost bereft of words.

"There isn't more than you'll need," Joan said encouragingly. "As soon as we know when you're starting, we'll bring them to King's Bottom and help you to pack them carefully. You'll like to show them to Mrs. Jaikes."

"When be we goin', Miss Joan?"

A look passed between the elder girls. Another interview with Boniface, after a night's rest for reflection on his part, had brought no better result. Indeed, Jen declared that she was sure he had wept all night.

"Because he wants to go so dreadfully much," she said sorrowfully. "If only he'd be brave and start!"

"We aren't quite sure, Vinny," Joan said

gravely. "Your Uncle Boniface doesn't seem to feel ready for the journey."

Lavinia turned wide dark eyes of dismay upon her.

"But he'll go, Miss Joan? I know he's an old 'un and he's feart; he said it to me. But you'd help us, and we'd get along all right. Uncle Bonny must come! I couldn't go on my lonesome!"

"Of course he'll come!" Jen cried, at sight of her distress. "We'll make him go! Don't look like that, Vinny! It will be all right! See what I've brought you for a good-bye present!" And she produced the string of brilliant red beads.

"Oh, Miss Jen! Them's beautiful!" Lavinia gasped. "Be they truly for me?"

"Take them home with you now, if you like. But don't lose them," Jen cautioned her. "You'll want to wear them with your new red dress. Susie, these are for you. They'll look pretty with that nice frock."

"Oh, Miss Jen!" Susie's cry of ecstasy went to Jen's heart.

"We can't leave you out of everything," she explained hastily. "You're a jolly good sort, Susie Spindle. Put on the beads and let us see how you look."

"Try on your red ones too, Lavinia," Janice suggested.

Overjoyed, the girls hung the chains round

their necks and admired the effect in the mirror Jen held before their delighted eyes.

"You both look very nice," Mrs. Shirley said, and they glanced at her gratefully.

"We'll tell you as soon as the date is fixed, Vinny," Joan promised. "We're going to have another talk with your uncle."

"Though what use it will be, I don't know," she said in despair, when Lavinia had gone, Susie escorting her part of the way, both chattering at full speed. "He seems quite unable to face the journey. That poor kid! What if we have to tell her she must go alone, after all?"

"On her lonesome," Jen added. "It would break her heart. If somebody's heart has to be broken, I don't see why it should be Vinny's. Can't we *make* Boniface go?"

"How, Jen, dear?"

"I've told you how," Joy remarked.

"Not your way. Couldn't we bundle him into the car and whizz him off to Southampton and put him on the ship by force?"

"I'm afraid we couldn't. We can only try to persuade him," Joan said despondently.

"You're very restless, Jandy Mac." Joy eyed Janice severely. "Is it worry over Boniface, or is there something on your mind?"

"I'm going to book my passage home. May I use your phone? I've been trying to decide on a date."

"Oh, Jandy! We don't want to lose you!" Joan

cried. "I know you have to go some day, but couldn't you put it off a little longer?"

"I've put it off several times already," Janice protested. "I had a letter from Alec this morning, and he thinks I ought to be starting for home."

"But you can't go till you've seen Boniface and Vinny safely off to Canada!" Jen wailed. "You've gone for voyages; you've sailed half-way round the world! You know all about ships. You almost made Boniface believe he could go. I was watching his face while you talked to him, and you nearly persuaded him. Oh, Jandy Mac, don't let us down! You're more likely to make him be sensible than anybody else!"

Joan and Joy looked hopefully at Janice. "Do help us through, Jandy!" they spoke together.

"I couldn't be ready for a week or two. Boniface will have to decide soon," Janice said. "There's a berth I can have in a fortnight; they told me so in town. I'll book that. Surely we'll be able to bring him to the point by then! I'd like to see him and Lavinia safely aboard. Don't look so blue, Joan! If the Babes in the Wood are still on our hands, I could cancel the berth and take my chance of another."

"That's the only reason I can think of for hoping Boniface won't give in!" Joan declared. "We don't want to lose you, Jandy."

"Dear knows when we'll see her again, once she's a married lady," Joy remarked. "I shan't do anything to hurry old Boniface!"

"We'll talk to him again. Perhaps we can coax him to be brave, for Lavinia's sake." But Joan did not sound hopeful.

They went back to the Abbey, firmly refusing to take Joy with them, in spite of her last assertion. She laughed and went to her piano. "Go without me, then! And good luck to your efforts. I'm not going to help to make the old chap go, if having him here will keep Jandy Mac here too. Let me know what happens!"

The three came back presently, disappointed and even more hopeless than before.

"It's not a scrap of use!" Jen wailed. "He just cries and says he'll stay here."

"He really was almost in tears," Joan said. "He keeps saying: 'If there was anybody else going, it would be different.' And that's quite futile."

"Send a courier with them," Joy suggested. "You can hire people to do it, I believe. A paid travelling-companion, who would see them safely into their friends' hands. I'll help to pay."

"That's generous!" Janice exclaimed, as if grasping at a new hope.

"But it wouldn't do, in this case," Joan said decisively. "Boniface and Vinny would be so terrified."

"They're terrified of everything," Joy said indignantly. "We'd choose somebody nice and homely, of course."

Joan shook her head. "It would be a stranger.

That wouldn't be any comfort to our Babes in the Wood."

"Do you mind if I go to bed?" Janice said abruptly. "I'm tired of Boniface. We've done all we can."

"Did you book that berth? Was it still available?" Joy asked.

"Yes, it's all right. I sail on the twenty-third."

"I shall be back at school," Jen said sadly. "I wonder where Boniface and Vinny will be?"

"Still where they are now. That old man doesn't mean to go, unless somebody will go with him to hold his hand." And Janice, disappointed and annoyed, went off to bed.

CHAPTER XXX

JANDY MAC IS NOBLE

"I want to talk to you three," Janice said.

Mrs. Shirley was breakfasting in bed, as she often did. Janice looked heavy-eyed, and Joan asked anxiously, "Didn't you sleep, Jandy?"

"Sorry you booked that passage? Don't you want to leave us?" Joy teased.

"Have you had an idea for Boniface and Vinny?" Jen pleaded. "Oh, Jandy Mac! Have you thought of something?"

"Jen's nearest." Janice pushed away her plate and spoke vehemently. "Listen, all of you! Would it help the Babes in the Wood, if I went with them as far as Montreal?"

"*Jandy Mac!*" There was a triple shout.

"How could you?" Joan cried. "You're going to Sydney!"

"Oh, if you only could!" Jen said longingly. "They like you. They'd love to go with you! But how could you go to Montreal?"

"Go home the other way, do you mean?" Joy looked at Janice with keen interest. "Through America and by the Pacific?"

"That's what I mean. There are two ways to Australia, Joan and Jen. I've always come by

238

Suez and the Mediterranean, but it's quite possible to go across America and by the Pacific. In Alec's last letter he suggested that I should go home that way and see our aunt and uncle in Montreal. Do you remember, when I came here to school last summer, it was because my aunt had gone to Canada to see her brother? I didn't go; I came here instead. I've never met the Canadian bit of the family, but Alec knows them, and he thinks it would be a good plan if I went and saw them before marrying and settling down. And then, he says, I'd come home through the Islands and get some idea where I'd like to live. We aren't going to stay in Sydney. His ship trades with Samoa and Fiji, and he's promised me a South Sea Island for our home. It all sounds very sensible, but——" and she paused.

"But you don't want to do it?" Joan looked at her closely. "When you booked your passage yesterday it was by the old route, I suppose?"

"The way I've always gone. I like it much better. I'm not keen on the Red Sea bit, but I do like to settle down on the ship and feel at home, knowing I needn't move till we reach Sydney Harbour. This other way will be interesting, even thrilling, but it's a lot more trouble, and I don't like the thought of the long train journey—days of it."

"Glorious trip! I shall go some day," said Joy, the roving spirit. "You'll have been right round the world! I envy you the chance."

"Did you really say Montreal?" Jen asked wistfully. "Oh, Jandy Mac, what luck! You could take Boniface and Vinny all the way! You'll do it, won't you?"

"I've been swithering all night!" Janice burst out.

"You've been what?" There was a stunned chorus.

"Swithering. Oh, sorry! It's one of my aunt's old words. Hesitating, then!"

"You booked your passage yesterday in a hurry, to have it settled." Joan understood. "But you hadn't quite decided, had you?"

"I shall feel utterly mean, and a frightful slacker, if I go by the easy route and leave those two lonely infants to find their own way to Montreal! Boniface is just a babe in arms when it comes to travelling. I could cancel the berth I booked and say I found I had to go by the other route. But——" and she paused again.

"Would it be very difficult? It sounds adventurous and complicated," Joan said anxiously.

"Uncle would see me through. He'd make arrangements about trains and the Pacific boats. No, it wouldn't be too hard. I should go straight to them; they live in Montreal. They'd see me on my way. And they'd like me to go; they've asked me more than once. They said, if aunty could do it, I could. I've always made excuses. But when I start I like to feel I'm going straight home, with no more changes and fuss. Going by

Canada, I shan't feel I have really started till I'm on the ship setting out to cross the Pacific." Her preference for the easy route was obvious.

"Think of all you'll see!" Joy said longingly. "The Rockies, and Niagara, and the Great Lakes, and the forests and prairies; and then those glorious islands in the Pacific! I don't know how you can hesitate!"

"Swither, was what she said. It's a useful word," Jen put in. "And talking about useful, think what a useful deed you'd be doing, by making the journey easy for Boniface and Lavinia, Jandy Mac!"

"Making it possible. They'll never go alone," Joy said.

"Could you bear it, Jandy?" Joan asked anxiously. "It would be so very kind!"

"Would it cost a great deal more?" Jen looked troubled. "With all those trains and things, I should think it might. It doesn't seem quite fair to Jandy Mac."

"That's decent of you, Jenny-Wren!" Janice exclaimed. "But I can afford it. Once I'm married at Christmas I shan't need to spend much for years. Living on a South Sea Island won't be terribly expensive."

"Your Alec would like you to go to Canada," Joy said.

"Yes, but Alec wouldn't like me to go second class," Janice retorted. "He insists I must go first, as I'm alone."

"Second class?" The inexperienced three looked at her blankly.

"But why?" Jen cried.

"Of course you'd go first, as usual," Joy exclaimed.

"Oh!" Joan said slowly. "Yes, I see. Boniface and Vinny would go second class; the cheques from their relations will only run to second. You feel you'd have to be with them. You are decent, Jandy!"

"Quite apart from the cheques, those two would be hopelessly out of place if they went first. They'd be terribly embarrassed and unhappy," Janice explained. "I know their people said they must come second and not steerage, and I think that's wise, for Boniface is old and may need to be looked after, and Lavinia's so desperately young. They're a weird couple! But first class wouldn't do for them at all. And do you think, any of you, that I could pretend to be taking care of them, and then when we reached the docks calmly say, ' Now, this is my part of the ship and that's yours, and I can come and speak to you, but you mustn't come to me '? Do you think I could be such a snob?"

"Of *course* you couldn't! You never would!" Jen cried.

"I shall tell Alec all about it when I get home, but in the meantime I shall have to keep it dark."

"Then you'll really do it?" Joy asked. "I'm

afraid I should want to swank in the first class. It's jolly nice of you! "

"Second class is all right. There's nothing wrong with it," Janice said. "I'm used to the other, but in this case there isn't any choice."

"I'm afraid there isn't. It's terribly good of you, Jandy," Joan said earnestly.

"I think it's perfectly noble!" Jen proclaimed. "To go the wrong way, and the wrong class, just for Boniface and Lavinia, is the noblest deed I ever knew!"

"Don't be mad!" Janice laughed indignantly. "The second class part is only for the first few days—just as far as Montreal. If I can't stand it for five or six days, I must be very hard to please. And I'm not. We shall be all right; you needn't worry about us. I rather hope Boniface will be a little sea-sick and have to lie down a good deal, so that Vinny and I can roam about together. I've an idea that Lavinia on a liner may be rather fun. And she's going to look quite presentable, thanks to you people. I shall tackle her English and give her lessons. She's quick, so she may speak quite well by the time we reach Montreal."

"She never says ' as how' now," Jen said eagerly. "You'll reform her, Jandy. I hope you will."

"People will think we're an odd crowd, but I can explain that I'm seeing the Babes in the Wood safely to their relations. Anybody can see they need it! I'll do it, Joan; I'm sure it's right. I'll give up Suez—not that I ever want to see Suez again! But it stands for the whole route. I'll go by the Rockies and the Pacific and choose my future home. Shall we tell Boniface? Or shall I phone and book the berths?"

"Let's tell him now!" Jen jumped up in excitement. "I want to hear what he says! Let's go at once! Oh, Jandy Mac, all our troubles are solved by your being so utterly noble and kind!"

"Jen, don't be an ass!"

"But it is kind," Joan said, more gently. "I don't know how to say all I feel, Jandy. We've a lot of jolly things by which to remember your visit, but this last is one of the very best. We'll never forget your kindness."

"What's that quotation about ' Nothing in life became him like his way of leaving it '? That's not right, but something like that," Joy said. "Jandy Mac has done a lot for us and given us a lot of things, but this—her way of leaving us—is quite one of the best."

"I'm not going to die!" Janice protested.

"It's the same thing, so far as we're concerned. You're going to be married, and you'll vanish to the other side of the world, and we shall never see you again. Oh, well! It's been very pleasant meeting you, Janice Macdonald!"

"Joy, don't be mad!" Joan exclaimed. "We shan't lose her. She'll write to us, and some day Jandy Mac will come back."

"Bringing a large and interesting family to

show us! But it won't be the same. And she'll forget to write."

"I hope you'll write to *me*. If you don't, I certainly won't write to you," Janice retorted.

"Come and tell Boniface! Never mind Jandy's future! I'm sure she'll come back some day. Come on, all of you!" And Jen raced to the door.

CHAPTER XXXI

THE BABES IN THE WOOD SET OUT

BONIFACE broke down in earnest, when at last he grasped what was going to happen.

"I wants to go terrible bad! Oh, Miss Joan, I does want to see my girl and the little 'uns! But I were feart o' that ship. If you'll be there too, Miss Janice, you as knows about ships, we'll be safe, Vinny and me. And I'll see my Annie and the grandchilder, and Vinny'll go to her dad. Oh, Miss Janice, I ain't got no words to tell you what I feels!"

"Then I'll go and make the arrangements," Janice said cheerfully. "Now, Boniface, Lavinia can be ready at any time. What about you? You haven't much packing to do, have you?"

"He needs a new warm overcoat, and a cap and scarf for the voyage," Joan said. "Ann Watson will pack for him; she has looked at his things, and they're in good order, and he has enough for the present. It's not like Lavinia, who had grown out of almost all her clothes. We must take him to Wycombe to buy a coat, but that's the chief thing he'll need. He has a good, strong trunk."

"Get him a big suitcase for the journey," Janice said, as they went back to the house, leaving Boniface, tremulous with joy and very great relief, to tell the news to Ann Watson. "I hope he'll retire to his bunk and stay there! I shall urge it on him; I feel Boniface may be a bit of a trial for five days on end. I'll ring up about berths, and we'll cable to Lavinia's dad to meet us, as soon as we know our dates. I'll write to the Montreal uncle, telling him I'm coming; and then we'll have an orgy of packing."

Lavinia's delight was as great as Boniface's had been.

"I didn' feel as how—oh, I'm sorry! I didn' feel Uncle Bonny would take care o' me prop'ly; he don't know nothing about ships. But Miss Janice, she knows it all. We'll be a' right with her. It's dreadful kind of her to go with us. Will she get home goin' our way?"

"Eventually," said Joy.

"Some day." Joan translated for Lavinia's benefit. "And she'll see her uncle and aunty, whom she doesn't know. That will be nice for her, won't it?"

"I don't see how anybody can expect me to go back to school to-night, with all this excitement going on," Jen grumbled. "As for thinking about lessons, I simply can't. You'll let me come to say good-bye to the Babes in the Wood, won't you?"

"They couldn't possibly go away without seeing you again," Joan assured her. "I shall come to school and tell Miss Macey the whole story, and beg her to let us have you for a day or two, when the travellers are on the point of sailing. And you're coming here for week-ends quite often, you know."

"You are nice to me!" Jen sighed contentedly. "I'm sure I don't know why! It will be horrible not having you at school. You had measles for most of last term; I think you should come back till Christmas, to make up for it."

"And leave Jandy on Mother's hands?"

"You could come when Jandy goes away. I know you know a lot, but I don't believe Joy does."

"Joy's going to work hard at music, and I'm going to look after Mother," Joan said. "It was because of her illness in the summer that we decided definitely not to go back to school. But I shall come often, to see how you're all getting on, and we'll always be at dance-evenings. I wonder who will be the next Queen?"

"Nesta," Jen said simply.

"You seem very sure about it! It's a long time till May."

"You wait and see. I know it will be Nesta. Everybody wants her."

"That's a good reason," Joan agreed.

"Old Beetle's going to be her maid. If she's chosen, Nesta'll be the Silver Queen."

"Nesta had better remember it's only ' if ', for a good many months yet. What flower would she choose, as a Silver Queen?"

"Honesty; the thing with white seed-pods, like silver pennies. But they won't show on a silver train, so she'll have a purple border, the colour of honesty flowers, and the silver pennies will be scattered along the edge. It sounds jolly fine."

"It's an original choice," Joan commented. "But Nesta shouldn't talk about it until she's really chosen Queen."

"Oh, she doesn't. She keeps on shutting us up. But we want her, so we talk about it."

"Don't overdo it!" Joan advised.

Janice, her mind at last made up, became her cheerful self again, and planned and worked, shopped for her trousseau and packed, and pored over maps and pamphlets from the steamship companies, driving Joy to wildest envy by her talk of the Rocky Mountains, the Canadian lakes and prairies and forests, and the lovely islands of the Pacific.

"If you don't take care, I shall throw over Aunty and Joan and come with you," Joy threatened. "I'm going round the world some day. I'll love to travel! I want to start at once. You're jolly lucky to be seeing so much at your age."

"I'll send you a picture postcard from the most beautiful place I see," Janice teased. "I wish we could start! I want to get my Babes in the Wood safely across before the autumn gales begin."

Jen, struggling with history and geometry at school and not in the least interested in either or in any other subject, came to the Hall for week-ends and entered into the excitement and heard all the plans, and joyfully examined Jandy's choice of clothes for her trousseau. Then, one great day,

Miss Macey sent for her and told her the car from the Hall would fetch her that afternoon.

"Oh, good! Are they going at last?" she cried, knowing that the Head understood.

"I believe they sail to-morrow," Miss Macey explained.

"Hop in, Jenny-Wren!" Joy opened the car door. "No time to lose! We didn't want to snatch you from your studies till the last moment."

"I wish you'd bagged me sooner." Jen sprang in beside her. "Is everything ready? When do they go?"

"Early to-morrow. We've sent off the luggage. I'm going to escort them to the docks and see them on board, because I'm dying to have a look at the ship."

"Can't we all go?"

"Joan won't come. She doesn't like tearful farewells in public, so she'll say good-bye at the house and stay with Aunty. You can do as you like, but if you come it will be a squeeze. We really ought to have a bigger car! You'll need to sit on Jandy's lap; I shall take Lavinia on my knee."

Jen considered the matter. "I'd like to see the ship, but I wouldn't like the good-byes; I agree with Joan. I shall stay with her."

"I'm tough; I shan't weep! But I'll be sorry to see the last of Jandy Mac."

"I suppose Vinny will come in the morning?"

"Vinny's going to tuck in with Susie for the

night; she's said good-bye to King's Bottom. You'll notice I don't say ' to sleep with Susie ', for I don't believe they will. Lavinia's in a state of wild thrills; they'll whisper all night. Uncle Bonny will come from the Abbey at eight o'clock; we're having very early breakfast. As for to-night——!" And Joy paused mysteriously.

"What about to-night? Anything special? Oh, Joy, tell me!"

"A farewell feast; a very high tea for the travellers and speeches in their honour. Then early bed for everybody."

"Oh, what a good idea! I'm glad you've asked me!"

"As if we could do without you!" Joy teased.

Lavinia, looking really pretty in her new red travelling-frock, and Boniface, very spruce in his best suit, were waiting to greet her at the Hall.

"We're goin' to-morrer, Miss Jen! Miss Janice'll take care of us on the ship," Vinny shouted, her face blazing with excitement. "See my red beads! Aren't they pretty?"

"There's a message from my Annie. She'll meet me at the other place." Boniface was tremulous with delight.

"A cable." Joan smiled at Jen. "Annie is so pleased he's coming. Now for tea!"

The very high tea was waiting, the table spread with all sorts of good things. Jen, fresh from school fare, delightedly did full justice to these, and Jandy's appetite was not in the least affected by the coming departure, but the other travellers were far too excited to eat much, though Lavinia's eyes glittered at sight of the heaped table.

"Just as well, perhaps," Janice murmured to Joy. "They'll probably be sea-sick."

Joan rose to say a few words of good wishes. Joy followed, prophesying a jolly voyage and a happy meeting with friends. Mrs. Shirley very quietly reminded everyone of Jandy's coming marriage and wished her every happiness in her new life.

"Hear, hear!" Jen cried. "I haven't prepared a speech, but I do hope you'll all be just terribly happy, and I'm sure and certain you will. Jandy Mac deserves all the happiness there is, and I expect she'll get it, though I don't see how her Alec can be half good enough for her." And she sat down, crimson and excited, while everybody laughed at Jandy's burning face.

Then an astonished silence fell, for Boniface Browning was on his feet. "I just wants to say ' thank you ' to all you kind folks," he quavered. "I'm so happy, right now, to be going to my girl that I got no words to say how I feels."

"Same from me!" Lavinia cried. "Thank you, Miss Joan and Miss Jen and Miss Joy and the lady, but most of all, thanks to Miss Janice for taking care of us."

"Well done, Lavinia!" Joan said. "Remember, all of you, that we want to have news of you, so you must write and tell us how you're getting on. We shan't forget any of you! Especially you,

Jandy Mac. Don't forget the Abbey when you settle down on your Island! Now off to bed, Lavinia! Back to the Abbey for one more night, Boniface! Don't be late in the morning!"

It seemed a very little while till the early breakfast, and then Joan and Jen stood on the terrace, waving as the laden car set out, and Susie hung from a bedroom window, shouting farewells.

When the car had disappeared down the beech avenue, Jen turned to Joan, her face radiant. "Aren't they all happy? Nobody cried! I wonder if we'll ever hear how they get on?"

"Jandy Mac will write. I don't expect much from Boniface or Lavinia."

"And now," Jen said impressively, "we shall have the Abbey all to ourselves again!"

Joan looked at her and smiled. "The Abbey has done its proper work, and the aged and infirm, and the very young, have been helped to make a fresh start. You and I are left to carry on at home," she agreed contentedly.

CHAPTER XXXII

THE BABES IN THE WOOD ARRIVE

To JEN's great delight, Jandy's letter about the voyage arrived at half-term. She was spending the long week-end at the Hall, so she enjoyed it with Joan and Joy.

"All went well," Janice wrote. "We had no difficulties. As I hoped, Boniface took to his bunk and stayed there; he wasn't very ill, but he was appalled by the size of the ship and the sight and sound of the sea, and he felt safer in bed. Lavinia was poorly for one day; then I made her get up, and once she went on deck she was all right. She loved it and enjoyed every minute—wanted to explore the ship, and could hardly take her eyes off the waves. She really was quite a jolly companion; her interest and delight in everything were so keen. And, by the way, she was talking much better before she escaped from my clutches. I kept on at her, pulling her up all the time—and she was eager to ' talk right ', as she put it, before she reached her father.

"We had a good voyage, quick and easy; no gales. Second class wasn't at all bad; I quite enjoyed it. Less fuss than in the first. At Montreal the relations met us, and I liked them all. Boniface's Annie seemed rather a dear, and she was so pleased to see her father! She brought the eldest grandchild with her, a fine boy of five, and Boniface's pride in his descendant was touching.

"Lavinia was nervous of her dad, but that didn't last long. He came himself, with one of her brothers, and I liked them very much indeed. They thanked me too; I felt myself getting hotter and hotter, with all the gratitude that was floating in the air! They said again that they hadn't meant to neglect Lavinia; they had thought she was happy at King's Bottom, and they couldn't see any way to get her to them, unless one of them came to fetch her, and that, I gathered, wouldn't have been easy, for the farm keeps them very busy. They are delighted to have her now. And I think they were pleased with her; they kept looking at her, as if they hadn't expected her to be so big, or so good-looking, or something. Her dad said she was very like her mother, so perhaps that was what he was thinking. She was shy, but she looked very pretty. I felt I was handing over something quite worth while! And there are two little half-sisters, called Molly and Bess, so Lavinia will be really useful. Her delight, when her father told her, was pathetic. She has been lonely; now she feels she has a family of her own.

"Then at last I was able to go off with Uncle Jim and Aunty. They really are awfully pleased to see me. I'm glad, now, that I came. They'll help me with the rest of the journey. It won't be difficult, they say, and it will be quite thrillingly interesting.

"Take care of yourselves, you dear people. I hope I shall see you all again some day. Give my love to Mrs. Watson and the Abbey; I expect you're enjoying having it to yourselves again. I am so very glad to have helped to restore it to you! Old Boniface won't come back; you can rest easy about that. He'll never face the ocean again! So the Abbey is yours, Joan and Jen, without any 'ancient spectre' appearing suddenly at the chapter-house door or toddling out of the sacristy!

"My love to you all. I shall come back some day.

"Yours ever,

JANDY MAC."

"A lovely letter!" Joan said happily.

"Nice to know the end of the story," Joy agreed. "Our Babes in the Wood are safe."

"It's jolly to think of Vinny taking care of Molly and Bess! She'll love them, and she'll be terribly kind to them. Perhaps we shall see them here some day. We must tell Susie," Jen said. "And the Abbey is really ours now! But I hope we'll see Jandy Mac again!"

Joan smiled at her. "She'll be Jandy Fraser next time we see her. But I'm sure our Jandy Mac will come back."